MW01148439

# BRIBING SAINT ANTHONY

## A MARY CATHERINE MAHONEY MYSTERY

## RITA MOREAU

Books by Rita Moreau

Bribing Saint Anthony

Nuns! Psychics! & Gypsies! OH NO!!

Feisty Nuns

The Russian & Aunt Sophia

Book design by George Moreau

Copyright © 2012 by Rita Moreau
First Edition June 2012
Second Edition November 2012
Originally published as Innocent Spouse

Copyright © 2014 by Rita Moreau
First Edition June 2014
Second Edition October 2017

*This book is dedicated to my mother, Georgia.*

*Your star shines bright in the heavens.*

CHAPTER 1

On one side sat 'blue blood, born rich,' who would never have to worry about money. On the other side sat 'gold digger, married rich more than once,' and any offspring would never have to worry about money. Cha-ching, cha-ching.

Each of these women had enough dough to single-handedly put a dent in the country's deficit, not to mention keep my small tax office afloat and eliminate any fear I ever had of having to move in with my aunts. Of course, without cultivating the psychic abilities I've been told I may possess, I failed to see the word 'disaster' spelled out in all caps on their wrinkle-free foreheads. Aunt Sophia would have clearly read, "Stop. Witch's Forest. Proceed, and you are toast."

I didn't need the family fortune-telling cards to tell me that across from my desk, sitting regal and upright, was the Queen Mother of Boca Vista, Babbs La-Fleur. Sitting right next to her sat the darling of Fish Camp, Jennifer Stone, aka the Queen of Hoochie Mommas.

On the alpha side sat Babbs: blond hair, patrician face, thin to the bone and dressed in casual rich. Not blinged-up rich, subdued rich. The type of rich you recognize after years of working at the IRS or Neiman Marcus.

Sitting next to Babbs on what appeared to be the hot seat was Jennifer Stone. Jennifer was genetically gifted by heaven at birth. Not with wealth, but with the other assets that would enable her to acquire all the wealth she would ever need and then some.

Although Jennifer was not as rich as Babbs, but was a close second, thanks to a series of lucrative, trophy wife marriages and the accumulation of the cash, alimony, and other assets acquired upon the dissolution of those marriages.

Jennifer, unlike Babbs, was not dressed in casual rich. She dressed in successful gold digger rich. Marilyn platinum blond hair piled high and teased in a throwback to the sixties beehive. She had the type of cleavage that could not be store bought and a figure way too petite for that cleavage, and jewelry, lots and lots of jewelry, expensive and flashy. No, there was nothing subtle about Jennifer Stone. She was, in a word, a Hoochie Mama. She loved NASCAR, honky-tonks and country music, and life in general, and karma returned the favor.

Queen Babbs came to life, took charge of the meeting and came right to the point.

"I understand you used to work for the IRS as an agent like my husband, Charlie. In fact, you may have known my husband when he worked for the IRS in Fort Lauderdale."

"Yes. I remember your husband, Charlie," I said with my best professional smile.

Actually, I knew all about Charlie, he was a bit of a

folk hero at the IRS. Charlie was a good man but also a bad boy. Rumor was that he married Babbs for her money. Between husbands and wives, Charlie and I had a short fling. That was the extent of polite small talk while I felt myself blush red from the memory.

"My husband, Charlie has disappeared," Babbs said. I listened while she paused to watch my reaction. Gathering from the look on my red face, she registered that this was news to me and she continued. I glanced at Jennifer who was busy admiring the rock on her manicured finger. No help there.

Babbs got out of the chair and walked behind Jennifer who, on cue, looked up from the rock.

"He left right after the tax season ended," Babbs said, both women now looking straight at me.

At that point, the professional smile started to fade, and I began to get an uneasy feeling that something else was going on here, and it was being orchestrated by these two women. I looked up and saw Velma out of the corner of my eye standing by my office door eavesdropping.

"Go on," I said to Babbs as I looked away from Velma and managed to flash a weak smile. Jennifer went back to her rock admiration. Babbs stood behind her chair and continued with the story.

"Charlie usually takes off for his annual fishing trip to the Keys to celebrate the end of tax season. He is usually gone for about a week or two, and it's not unusual if I don't hear from him until he is heading back. When one week went by and then another, and I still had not heard from him, I started to worry," Babbs said while glancing over at Jennifer who looked as if she had stopped breathing momentarily.

"Through information I had obtained by way of a contact, I had Bruce, my personal assistant, contact Jennifer and determine if she had any information related to his whereabouts," Babbs said while my brain was working to keep up and process this information. She then looked directly at Jennifer who immediately looked up at me while placing her hands on her lap. The rock probably was getting heavy.

"What you may or may not know is that Charlie and Jennifer were having an affair," she said without blinking.

Jennifer looked up and took a deep breath and said, "Ms. La-Fleur, that is nothing but pure fantasy dreamed up by Bruce. I've told you before, and I'll tell you again, Charlie is my CPA, and that is the extent of our relationship. Bruce needs to stop playing the drama queen and inventing gossip."

Bruce was the Queen's personal assistant by title, pretty much Babbs's everything else. He was her chauffeur, her bodyguard, her food tester, her appointment handler, her personal shopper, and when needed, he even managed crowd control. It was no secret that he was her closest confidant.

Babbs shot her a queenly and authoritative look, which was basically the evil eye, which Jennifer returned in kind. Babbs decided to ignore Jennifer's protests and directed her attention back to me waiting for a response.

Wisely, I didn't say a word and was only wondering why we were having this gabfest in my office. It seemed more suited over a glass of wine at the local watering hole, and not my small tax and accounting office. I shot a quick sideways glance at Jennifer when Babbs took a minute to blink her eyelashes. Jennifer just looked at me with a blank slate on her face giving me no clue. Out of the corner of my eye, I could see Velma still at the door eavesdropping.

"The specifics of the affair are immaterial," Babbs said as if she was dismissing and filing that report away. "I suspected it, and although I did not condone it, I accepted it. After all, I am a number of years older than Charlie," Babbs said with another batting of the eyelashes.

Out of the corner of my eye, I caught Jennifer rolling her eyes so far back that for a split second I thought I was going to have to get Velma to call 911. When I glanced at her, the blank slate was back.

"When Bruce and Jennifer talked, she told him that she had not heard from Charlie either and was also worried about him," Babbs said. We both looked over at Jennifer who continued to admire the rock that she had moved to the other well-manicured hand.

Jennifer sensed the stare and looked up and said, "Yes, that's correct," as if on cue but still eyeballing the rock, and then she added, "the part about not hearing from Charlie, but not the affair. Bruce, the drama queen, got that part right," she said giving the rock a rest while looking straight at me.

Babbs just stared at Jennifer, let out a long sigh, shook her head as if dealing with a problem daughter, and then turned her attention back to me.

"Ms. Mahoney, I will get right to the point. I would like you to find Charlie," and then with real emotion, she added, "I don't care what he has done, just tell him to come home and all is forgiven."

I noted that Babbs said 'I would like you' as if giving me a direct order, as opposed to the normal 'I would like to hire you' I usually hear from my clients. The Queen thing. It was now my turn to speak. Those two were all of sudden quiet and were both staring at me. It was a little unsettling and reminded me a bit of some of the family meetings I've had in the past with my mother and aunts. Jennifer had even stopped with the adoration of the rock on her finger and was giving me her undivided attention, once again, almost as if on cue.

"Ladies, to begin with, please call me Mary Catherine or MC for short," I said to them.

"Ms. La-Fleur, you seem a little confused. The services that I offer are accounting and tax related."

And then I added, " It sounds like what you really need is a private detective." Fishing for a clue as to what was really going on here, I added, "If you do not want to report this to the police."

"Call me Babbs, dear," she said, and then waited for my response. "You, too," she directed the command to Jennifer, who smiled back and silently mouthed "Okay."

I then proceeded to stick my foot in my mouth. "Granted, I have done some investigative accounting, but—"

"That is why I am here, MC," she said, now on a first name basis as she rose regally out of the seat and reached across the desk and patted my hand. I immediately sensed those two had set me up and were waiting for those words to open the door.

"I am aware of your reputation with the IRS as an investigative accountant. I think your job title was a Strike Force Agent," she said as she pointed her finger at me, not unlike my mother used to do…scary.

"I have been told that when it came to investigative accounting, you were the best at the IRS." Babbs was now walking over to the window while I sat trying to get my foot out of my mouth.

I watched her and then I saw what caught her eye. It was Izzy, sitting on the window ledge looking back at her with his sweet, little iguana smile.

"What an unusual creature," Babbs said when she reached the window. "Personally, I feel sorry for the plight of the iguanas and do not condone the town's zeal to eliminate their population. I'll make a note to follow up with Bruce on this issue," she said regally.

I walked over and smiled at Babbs, and at the same time I tapped on the window with my 'get the heck out of here' look, but Izzy stood his ground. *Great. Now, I'm going to have to talk to Velma about Izzy.*

I smiled at Babbs again, gave Izzy a quick sneer, and went back to my desk. I guessed that Charlie had told Babbs about my job at the IRS as a Strike Force Agent and my skills as an investigative accountant. Granted, the desperate housewives in town had discovered that I could track down their husband's hidden assets, but this woman knew something more than that about me and my work at the IRS.

"That's why I came to you," Babbs said smiling back at Izzy and making her way back to her chair.

"I was told by good sources that if anybody could find Charlie, it would be you. That you could find Charlie exactly the same way the IRS got Al Capone."

*Great, the barn door is wide open, and the animals are out.* I just sat there in a pile of manure while she continued.

"I am prepared to give you access to all our financial records, bank accounts, credit cards, tax returns, etc. You can use those to trace my husband's whereabouts. Keep looking through those books and records until you locate him." Babbs paused for a second and added, "I tried a detective, but…let's just say it did not work out."

Babbs was now standing behind Jennifer, and they were both staring at me while I stalled to gather my thoughts. It was a little disconcerting. These two women were staring at me like cats waiting for the prey (me) to make a move. *Who in the heck had referred Babbs to me?*

"Okay, okay," I heard myself saying and stalling as best as I could. "So, you want me to go through your financial records to track Charlie down and determine his whereabouts?"

"Yesss," Babbs said stretching out the "s" while arching her eyebrows, which were strangely not moving upwards. Jennifer was sitting upright in front of her smiling back, and the beehive had started to bounce up and down. I expected bees to fly out at any moment. Taken off guard by the eyebrows and the bee hive, Babbs jumped in before I could say anything and said, "I always kept detailed records, even before I married Charlie." Of course, she did, I thought. This woman was no dummy.

"In fact, I've kept up my personal financial records even after our marriage. Charlie assisted my Uncle Sal with the business since our marriage and also maintained his tax practice. I met Charlie when looking for a CPA firm for the business. Up until then, running the family grocery business and everything that went along with that had been done by my Uncle Sal. But, he is getting older and not in the best of health," Babbs said.

"He kept his tax business records separate, but I have access to those, also, if you need them." And then she added, "I have a key to his office and can arrange for Bruce to take you there." She then wrapped up the speech.

"MC, you will have whatever you need at your disposal to find Charlie, whatever it takes. Whatever I own, consider it yours. I just want Charlie found and brought home," Babbs said to me and to Jennifer, who was now taking on the role of the dutiful daughter. Jennifer nodded at Babbs and flashed me one of her movie star smiles.

I was now sitting there with a full-blown hot flash. This had nothing to do with taxes and accounting. Glancing over at Jennifer I suspected that she was more involved than she was letting on. Velma had slipped out and gone back up front.

I started to say without much conviction, "Well, I don't know. Like I said, it's really a job for a private detective and, I'm sorry to say, possibly the police."

At that moment Babbs, still standing behind her, tapped Jennifer on the shoulder and said, "Jennifer," and pointed at her purse.

Jennifer, on cue, reached down and handed Babbs

her very expensive Prada purse. A purse that I knew cost more than the entire wardrobe sitting in my closet. Babbs opened the purse and took out a stack of cash about an inch high and handed it to Jennifer, who seemed, by instinct, to know what to do with cash. She placed it neatly in the middle of my desk.

Silent once again, these two women were staring at me watching for my reaction. *Cash.* I was mesmerized by it sitting squarely in the middle of my desk, an imaginary line between these two women and me. I knew if I picked it up, I would be crossing over the line to the other side and whatever these two had waiting for me. This is where the Witch's Forest sign began to blink like a neon sign.

"Ten thousand dollars," Babbs said and added, "just to take the case, a retainer."

I sat there without moving or saying anything. CPAs are not used to such big retainers. That kind of money belonged to the high-powered, sleazy attorneys of the criminal tax world.

Babbs tapped Jennifer's shoulder again and pointed to the magical purse. I watched as Jennifer pulled out an even larger stack of cash and lined it up next to the stack sitting in the middle of my desk.

"Would five thousand dollars a week plus expenses do?" Babbs looked at me as if she was negotiating redecorating a vacation home, and then she added the closer.

"Whatever is mine is yours, my planes, cars, home and my entire staff."

I sat there in disbelief. The little voice in my brain was shouting at me by now, trying to tell me that this was more than a woman looking for a husband who had been gone a little longer than usual. But the cash on my desk was mesmerizing.

The office was still. Babbs had sat down, and both women were waiting across from my desk for an answer. They were staring at me like we were playing a game of poker, and by the looks on their perfect faces, they knew they had the winning hand.

By now, I wasn't watching the Witch's Forest sign or listening to the little voice in my head because all I could hear was the deafening sound of cha-ching…cha-ching. No worries for a while about paying bills, and best of all, no fear of having to move in with Aunt Sophia and Aunt Anna. I was hooked.

As I took a breath, Babbs, as if reading my mind, said, "Draw up the engagement letter and bring it to my house tomorrow. I will have Bruce call today to set up a time and go over any details. We will get you all set up in an office to start going over the records." And with that, she reached over again and tapped my hand as if to say, "Don't worry, dear, it will be all right."

My brain was working at warp speed as they both got up to leave. Oh brother. I knew the cash was the lure that hooked me, but I also knew that I was also just plain curious about what was up with Charlie, and what was really behind this search for him by these two women. Curiosity had always been my Achilles heel, and at the same time, it was what had made me so good at investigative accounting when I worked at the IRS.

"Well, I guess I could look into it," I said as I tried to muster some professionalism back into the meeting.

*What harm could come out of it?* It's amazing how the rationalization process kicks in as soon as you know you've made the wrong decision.

I was already working the plan out. I would take a look at the books and records, put my best investigative accounting to work and get a lead on Charlie, who was probably down in the islands sipping rum. Then I would set up a meeting with the PI Babbs had hired. The PI could take it from there, pick up the trail, track down Charlie in no time, and have him home by dinner on one of those private planes. I could just picture that homecoming.

They were now quickly making their way out of the office. Jennifer stood, held the door and waited for Queen Babbs to exit, again playing the role of the dutiful daughter, when I woke up and said, "I will need the name of the private investigator you hired so I can arrange a meeting."

Babbs turned and looked at me with the cool demeanor of one who was holding the winning cards and now was showing her hand. "His name was Harry

West. But, he was found dead," she said. "Shot. You may have read about it in the newspapers." With that, the Queen turned to Jennifer, shaking her head, and heaving one big sigh.

Jennifer handed her the magic purse and waited to follow. Jennifer turned back and looked at me with an expression on her face that said, "I'm sorry" and then followed Babbs out of my office.

"Dead?" I said. Both women turned back to look at me with an expression on their flawless faces and sly smiles that said, "Is there any other way?" *Snookered!*

I sat there unable to move. I had taken the bait, hook line and sinker, and had just been reeled into the boat by Captain Babbs and her First Mate, Jennifer. I was now oblivious to the cash sitting on my desk as I heard Babbs going out the front door and Jennifer exchanging a few words with Velma.

I got up, still in a daze, and walked out to the front office as Jennifer went out the door. Velma was just sitting there waiting to see the grand exit. We both walked to the window and watched as Bruce, wearing his chauffeur's uniform and cap, closed the door of the big, old black Rolls for Babbs, clicked his heels and got behind the wheel and took off.

As soon as the Rolls left we heard the roar of the Corvette engine fire up, watched the top roll down all on its own, and in a split second, there was a flash of red followed by blond hair flying in the wind.

Something told me that both of those women were now wearing contented smiles. Babbs, in the back of her Rolls, probably sipping champagne and eating bonbons, telling Bruce all about the meeting; and Jennifer, with her radio blaring, singing along to country music, as she flew down the road.

To make matters worse, Izzy had slipped in through the front door and was now making his way to his perch on top of one of the filing cabinets in a closet I had converted for files when I had set up the office. I turned to Velma as I started back into my office and said, "You know, we really have to do something about that iguana."

She ignored me, following me into my office, but stopped cold and looked at the cash sitting on my desk.

"Whoa, I didn't know those fancy purses came with cash, too," she said.

"Neither did I," I said as we both stared at the cash like it was going to sit up and start talking to us.

"How much?" Velma asked.

"Ten thousand and change," I heard myself saying.

"I'd say it's more like twenty thousand," Velma replied.

"Really?" I said looking up at Velma and then back at the two wads of cash sitting on my desk.

"Um hum," Velma said.

"There's only one way to find out for sure," and with that Velma reached down and grabbed a wad and started counting the cash.

"Lock the front door," she said not looking up at me.

I went up front to lock the door and turned to see Izzy behind me, heading into my office. I walked up, stopped in front of him, looked down and said, "stay." He looked up at me and hearing the tone in my voice, turned around and headed back to his perch.

"Good boy," Velma said without turning around as I went back in and watched her pick up the second stack and finish counting.

"Finally," I said, "how much?"

Velma now had that smile on her face that she usually reserved for her favorite, cheesecake.

"Twenty-five thousand," Velma said.

"You need to get this to the bank," Velma said as we went up front for something to carry the cash in, and then came back to start scooping the bills into plastic bags from Wal-Mart. "After that, we can talk about your meeting with the Queen."

I came back to life, grabbed my dusty gym bag sitting in the corner, and after spilling its contents on the floor, stuffed the Wal-Mart bags into it. I felt an urgency to get this much cash to a safe place.

"Ok, I'm going," I said to Velma as I stood there

with my gym bag like I was heading for a workout.

"We will also be talking again about that raise," Velma added. She definitely had that cheesecake smile on her face.

"After the bank, I have to go talk to Ernie and try to get a handle on this," I said as I started to make my way out of the office.

"Ernie? Are you nuts?" Velma said following me. "You're a CPA, not a spook, and Ernie is a spooky spook."

"Well, he's not really a spook, he worked for Homeland Security," I said.

"Homeland Security is the black hole for spooks. Trust me, that man was and *is* a spook," Velma said.

I thought about this for a minute while Velma headed out of my office to unlock the front door.

Velma had been privy to a lot of stuff in her position in Marathon, and before that, in the IRS office we worked at in Fort Lauderdale, where I had honed my investigative accounting skills. But where did she get a handle on how much cash was sitting on my desk? I put that thought on hold and opened the door to leave.

"Yeah, okay, I know, but it looks like folks around here think that since I worked for the IRS, and since CIA, FBI, and IRS are all three-letter words, that the jobs are synonymous. Anyway, I have a funny feeling he was the one who referred Babbs to me in the first place, otherwise, how would she have known about my investigative background with the IRS? I want to find out why and what he knows about this PI of hers that was found shot dead."

So, I went out the door and headed to the bank with the dough. I looked back to see Velma waving good-bye, and Izzy sitting right there next to her as Velma closed the door. Snap!

CHAPTER 2

I managed to get to the bank and carefully placed the cash into my safe deposit box, which I had opened when I first launched my office. It was a family tradition to have a safe deposit box at the bank.

I think it went back to the era my mother and aunts had grown up in; "depression babies" they would say. "Don't put all your money in the bank just in case it goes under," and "Always put some away in a safe deposit box for a rainy day, along with a bottle of good ouzo for good luck." I could hear my mother's words in my head.

I'd had many a conversation with my mother where I attempted to explain to her that money was safe in the bank, and, oh, by the way, safe deposit boxes are always located in the bank! It was useless; she listened with that 'you will find out someday' look. I guess she was right, because, as I get older, I am finding more and more, because here I was, placing more cash than I've ever had at one time in my lifetime in my safe deposit box. And in this current economy, I'm not so sure I don't want to keep it under the mattress, which is where my grandmother had kept her emergency fund.

Right now, I was glad I had followed the family tradition and had the safe deposit box because I wasn't quite ready to make a deposit of $25,000 in cash until I got a better handle on this case. And today the ouzo looked very inviting.

I had rationalized in my head, on the walk back from the bank to my car, that I would probably end up keeping some of the cash, a reasonable fee plus triple damages for the headaches and weight gain this woman was about to cause me while I was out and about looking for Charlie. I would then return the balance to Babbs.

I did not want to be tied at the hip to Queen Babbs, which is what would happen if I kept all the cash. I believed that becoming her personal private eye/accountant was what Babbs had in mind when she slapped that sizable cash retainer on my desk today.

I certainly wasn't interested in that job, especially since I, no doubt, would be taking orders directly from the Queen Bitch, Bruce. No wonder Charlie was missing in action.

My plan at the moment was that I would do enough work to get a lead on Charlie's whereabouts and turn that information over to Babbs. She could then turn the whole matter over to another PI to locate Charlie if he was still MIA. At least that was my plan for now while I also pondered the elephant sitting in the room: whether or not the demise of Harry West, PI, was related to Charlie's disappearance.

Velma called my cell to say Bruce had phoned and set up an appointment in the morning for me to meet with Babbs at the mansion. Since I couldn't talk to

Babbs' detective, I decided to do the next best thing and pay a visit to Ernie, despite Velma's warnings.

I hopped in my car and drove along the beach. It was a beautiful summer day, and I was thankful for the fresh air after the meeting with Babbs and Jennifer. Plenty of sunshine and right now no hurricanes on the horizon. The snowbirds had all departed, and the beach had been reclaimed by locals.

Up ahead I could see the tiki bar, and although it was barely noon, it was packed with locals and regulars grabbing a bite and drinks. Right smack in the middle was Ernie tending bar.

I parked my car in between two rows of Harleys which made the parking lot look like bike week in Daytona. I made my way through a throng of bikers who hung out regularly at Hotel Florida, along with the spooks. We all lived in a postcard. Having settled in paradise, some for a short time and some for life, all of us have become pirates at some time in our lives. It was true.

Ernie spotted me and pointed me to a seat at the bar. "Well, what brings you here today? Have you decided to retire from the CPA life, or is your Frankenstein Abby Normal brain still in control?"

Ernie and I usually had a few minutes of running dialogue as to why I was still working in the tax field and had not taken the buyout from the IRS to open a new chapter in my life. I usually told him I never learned to tend bar. That took care of that conversation until the next time.

I knew Ernie from my days with the IRS. His employer, whoever that was, assigned him to work on joint task forces with the IRS and the Department of Justice. I had met him years ago while working as a Strike Force Agent on cases looking first into organized crime and money laundering and then after 9/11, terrorists.

I could usually find Ernie at Hotel Florida, an outdoor tiki bar on the beach, where he worked part-time as a bartender. Ernie told newcomers that he was retired from Homeland Security and tended bar to have something to do. He wasn't ready for the rocking chair. For a man close to 70, he looked good, a cross between Willie Nelson and Clint Eastwood.

For some reason, after Ernie arrived, the tiki bar seemed to attract what Velma calls the local spooks, cops, PIs, IRS, FBI and all the types I thought I left behind with my old job. But, we weren't that far from Lauderdale or Miami, both a mecca of spooks, pirates, crooks and Hollywood types. So you never knew who was hanging out at the Hotel Florida tiki bar. I usually recognized a few faces at the bar, sometimes it was just like old home week.

From time to time Ernie would disappear for a few weeks or months. I suspected he was occasionally called back to work by that spook agency.

I had decided to use Jennifer as bait to get a handle on this case and to confirm my suspicion that he was the one who sent Babbs to my office and to find out why. I knew if I mentioned her name he would go brain dead for a short while. Here was someone who had led the secret agent life and maybe even had the president's ear, but all that melted into a teenage boy with a monster crush when her name was mentioned. I waited patiently while Ernie poured a few more margaritas for the biker crowd.

He beat me to the punch. This was going to be easier than I thought. "I happened to see Jennifer Stone the other day at the Boca Vista recreation center. She was coming out of that Zumba class you told me you attend." Jennifer, upon reaching the first milestone of aging, thirty, joined the rest of us women at Zumba.

"You sound like you are stalking her," I said as I took a sip of my beer. I couldn't resist the jab.

"MC, if I wanted to stalk her, I would employ more discreet tactics than hanging around outside a Zumba class," he said and then continued. "I am happy to report since working out at the recreation center I feel better than ever. Might even get up the courage to talk to Jennifer next time I see her."

Yeah right, I thought, as I took another drink of the cold beer. He was in great shape and commanded the respect of the younger crowd that frequented Hotel Florida. Early on, he taught a couple of them a lesson, and from that day on, nobody messed with Ernie.

"Ernie, there's something I'd like to ask you that actually involves Jennifer." You would have thought I told him where he could find a buried treasure. He was staring at me as if we were the only two around, and I was holding the treasure map.

"Shoot," he said. Not wanting to waste any time because I wasn't sure how long this transformation was going to last, I took a quick swig and ventured on.

"Generally, I don't disclose client dealings, but I'm a little out of my comfort zone on this one and may need your input."

I told him about my meeting with Babbs and Jennifer including the murder of the private investigator, Harry West. He didn't seem surprised about any of it, or even that Jennifer was part of the meeting.

"I would like to get a lead on the paper trail Charlie left without winding up dead like Babbs's PI," I said, and then waited for his reply.

"I see," he said, and then he followed up with, "On it."

"I'll look into it and come by your office to let you know what I've found." And then he added, "Of course, a chance meeting with Jennifer, which you could arrange, might be helpful."

*Okay, this is progress.* I wanted to say, "Ernie, you need to get in line and it's a long line." Instead, I said,

"I think that could be arranged. I'll wait to hear from you and let you know what I find out tomorrow after my meeting with the Queen at her mansion."

Since he still seemed to be in the ozone with thoughts of Jennifer and his lack of reaction to the shooting of Babbs's PI, I added, "By the way, you wouldn't happen to have known her PI, Harry West, the one that was murdered, did you?"

Ernie thought for a moment and then opened up like a clam.

"MC, I haven't been entirely upfront with you. Yes, I did know Harry West, and, yes, I confess I was the one who pointed Babbs in your direction." There it was, I wanted to yank that Willie Nelson ponytail out of his head, but instead held on to my beer bottle.

"Harry West was an old friend of mine from the … uh, old days. Bruce dropped by one day and told me that Babbs was worried because Charlie was overdue from his annual fishing trip to the Keys. I suggested to Bruce that you might be the right person to help locate Charlie. Awhile back, Charlie had dropped by for a few beers, and right as he was leaving asked me for the name of a PI, something to do with the grocery business. I sent him to Harry West. He was also retired from Homeland Security and working locally as a PI.

Just between us, I thought that, along the way, you might uncover some information so I could find out what happened to my friend, Harry West."

"Gee, thanks," I said as I heard the anger rise in my voice.

"So now, I am not only looking for," as I lowered my voice, "Charlie, who's probably still sipping rum out in the islands, but I might also be smack dab in the hunt to find out who killed your old friend Harry West."

Ernie took a minute to process this reaction from me and said, "Look, I was going to sit down with you and go over this, but since you're already here, just know that I am going to work with you on this."

He leaned over the bar and then whispered to me, "I have your back. You just do your part with the books and records, and I'll take care of the rest. Just like when you worked for the IRS."

With that, the meeting ended, and he went back to fixing drinks for the bikers. I sat there just like I had the other day after those two women left my office.

Ernie seemed to read my mind; he brought me another cold beer, smiled and said, "It's on the house," as I glared when he handed me the beer.

"Okay, I will talk to you later," I responded. He just gave me one of his smiles and walked off to tend bar. It was late, so I decided to head home.

Exhausted, I plopped into bed and had a dream about Izzy and his whole family of iguanas populating my office. I think Velma was in there somewhere feeding them cheesecake.

CHAPTER 3

I was curious where Charlie was, I suspected that the guy was up to no good. My Greek nose was twitching. For all I knew, it wouldn't surprise me that Charlie decided to hang it up to become a boat captain offering full-time sport fishing on the high seas.

The problem with the 'Charlie fishing on the high seas' scenario was the mystery surrounding the PI's death. Ernie said that Charlie had hired Harry West to do some work for the grocery business and Babbs then put him on Charlie's trail when he didn't return from his fishing trip to the Keys.

I don't believe in coincidences. Was there a tie between the murder of PI Harry West and Charlie's disappearance? Obviously, there was, or Ernie wouldn't be involved. "Just like when I worked at the IRS." This was not sounding good.

By introduction, my name is Mary Catherine Mahoney, MC for short. I grew up in Fish Camp, a small Florida town, in a big, fat, Greek family where I also survived St. Mary's parochial school. We were the only Greek family in town who were Catholics or vice versa, whichever way you wanted to look at it.

When it came time to be christened, my mother along with my Aunt Sophia, my Aunt Anna and the rest of the family bundled me up in the family christening outfit. They took me to the Greek church in the next town over, Boca Vista, where the Greek priest refused to baptize me as soon as he found out that my dad wasn't Greek, but a WASP and a country-music-loving red-neck, to boot.

Fish Camp and Boca Vista sit side by side but are as different as spare buttons in a sewing box. Two Florida towns that grew up along Florida State Road A1A in the days when Florida was the tourist attraction of the U.S. Boca Vista aspires to be another Palm Beach, and Fish Camp is quite content as a smaller version of Nashville.

Never one to let protocol get in the way, as soon as the family got back home, my mother went down the street and joined St. Mary's, a beautiful but old Catholic church falling on hard times in our middle-class neighborhood. In Fish Camp, most of the residents were Baptists.

There the priest, Father Bob, for a fee collected from the family and some carpenter work my dad agreed to do for the church, was glad to see that I was properly baptized.

The important thing to my mom, the matriarch and backbone of the family, was not what church you showed up at on Sunday, but to get me baptized in case I didn't make it through my formative years. Deeply spiritual and just as superstitious, she didn't want her firstborn child running around loose in Limbo.

Over the years, she would debate the story with her

two sisters, Sophia and Anna. It always led to the same discussion, the same argument and the same head shaking and eye rolling by my two aunts. The fact that my mother changed her religion overnight from a long line of Greek ancestors just to ensure my christening was baffling to my spinster aunts.

"Greek, Catholic, Jewish, what difference does it make?" My mother would say to my aunts. "You don't need a church or a religion to talk to the big man in the sky. That door is always open, only you can close it. I changed where I show up on Sunday, not my beliefs."

That was the difference between the three women whose roots I share; my mother's beliefs were rooted in spirituality while my aunts were tied to organized religion. I tend to follow my mother in that respect.

About the time I was to enter high school, Dad had St. Mary's nearly restored to her to prior glory (much to Father Bob's delight). But then Dad while working on the statue of St. Joseph, which stood right next to the main altar toppled off a ladder and broke his neck.

Father Bob gave him a great send-off and a funeral mass even though Dad had never converted to Catholicism. After a conversation that took place in the confessional one morning between my mother and Father Bob, my tuition was waived for my remaining time at St. Mary's parochial grade school, and after that at the all-girls Catholic high school, Mary Help Us.

A few years later, I flunked out of college. I had

decided I had sat through enough school; I wanted my independence and a job more than a college diploma. Only later did I learn that college diplomas led to a job and my independence.

My mother, along with my Aunt Sophia and Aunt Anna, sat me down at the family dining room table along with the family fortune-telling cards, Greek coffee spiked with who knows what, probably ouzo, and then called a family meeting, the three of them and me.

I knew it was serious because after the reading of the cards they placed me on the couch covered with plastic shrink wrap, the one usually reserved for funerals or heads of state. I sat there perspiring and sticking to the couch while the three of them hovered over me.

They were wearing their power suits: Sunday going-to-church dresses, black pumps, and gray hair pulled back in tight buns. My mother, as always, spoke for the three.

"We think you should get a job now," my mother said with a nod of her head in my direction, squinting her dark eyes and then taking a dramatic pause for the lifting of one of her equally dark eyebrows.

"Probably one where you won't get fired right off the bat," she added with a little more emphasis and the dreaded pointing of the pointer finger.

My mother's pointer finger was well used, mainly

on me. This was followed by another pause and an amazing display of nodding heads, squinting eyes and arching eyebrows, all in unison.

"A nice government job," my mother finished. That was the message.

They finished the meeting with the three of them standing before me, hands clasped together in front, now smiling accompanied by more head nodding. They looked like three bobble dolls, but I got the point. After that, they fed me, and then read the family fortune cards just to make sure.

Usually, I was not one to take their advice. I just never bought into the whole reading of the family fortune-telling cards. I decided that maybe I should at least consider it, especially since college was no longer a viable option.

So, I took a typing and shorthand course, passed the government civil service test and found myself working for the Internal Revenue Service (or the Infernal Revenue Service, as it's known in some circles), in Fort Lauderdale.

It wasn't difficult to land a job with the IRS at that time. The Democrats were in office, so government jobs were plentiful, plus most of their newly hired workers usually quit after the first year. Working for the IRS has a way of isolating one from the rest of the human population. Not everyone can handle that.

While working for the IRS, shunned by the human

population and all, I settled down, got serious and went back to school and finished with an accounting degree. Miraculously, after the allotted number of tries, I managed to pass the CPA exam.

So, I settled into a safe government job, and snap, twenty-some years of my life gone, working for the IRS before I even knew it. Then one day out of the blue I was offered a bribe, not by someone whose audit I was handling, but to my surprise, by my employer.

The bribe was called a buyout, but first, it came with the news that my job was being abolished because the IRS office I worked at in Marathon, Florida, was being closed down.

What is up with that?" I thought at the time. Who would have thought the government actually closed offices, especially the IRS? So, it wasn't as if I even had a choice in the matter. Times had changed, and the Republicans were in office.

I left Fort Lauderdale saying good-bye to my safe, but stressful and thankless job, and came home to Fish Camp, where my mother and two aunts were waiting. Leaving the IRS before retirement age led to a Cat 5 storm that night around the family dinner table.

I sat there and did my best to explain to my mother, while my aunts listened, about the events that led up to my job being abolished and the buyout.

I was still trying to sort it out in my head. I was even starting to wonder if the buyout had anything to do with one of the last cases I worked on at the IRS. The Marathon office was small and removed from the big IRS office in downtown Miami since we handled sensitive cases that had ties to possible terrorist activity or mob involvement.

As we sat around the family dining room table loaded with enough food to ensure my appearance on one of next season's reality shows, my mother dropped the bomb, "So did you get fired?" I wasn't surprised; I knew it was coming.

My Aunt Sophia gave her a look, but then all six eyes were on me and maybe their third eyes also.

"No, Mother," I said. "I did not get fired. It was a buyout. My job was abolished when the office I was working in was closed, and when that happens, the government offers you a buyout. There's a lot of that going on now, you know, with the economy and all," I said.

This was a lame explanation, and I knew she didn't buy it because I didn't buy it. But it seemed to placate her, and she dropped it. But I knew she would get back to it when she found the right moment. She was patient like that.

"They didn't offer you another job?" she asked after dinner as we took the dishes to the kitchen. Picking up the conversation where it left off as if an entire meal hadn't happened in between.

"No, Mother, they didn't." I looked at her, and we

seemed to both think about the fact that they had not offered me another job.

"Hmm," she said, and walked into the kitchen to wash the dishes with my aunts, even though they had a dishwasher.

"Something else must have happened, you were too good at your job," she said. "You must have ruffled some feathers," she said as she pointed a soapy dish at me while I watched the soap drip on the floor next to her bare feet. My mother never wore shoes unless she had to and never in the condo she shared with my two aunts.

I was a little steamed at my mother's suggestion that I ruffled some feathers. I almost always assumed I knew better than her, a little old Greek lady who believed in fortune tellers and a deck of fortune-telling cards, which she would tell me she could read the same as I read a set of financial statements.

It was a gift from above, she would say, pointing her finger at me while I gave her the "yeah sure" look. "You have that gift, but you choose to ignore it."

Later that night, when I couldn't sleep I took a deep breath and allowed myself to cave into her line of thinking.

In the dark, I first conceded she might have been onto something. Once I got that out of the way, I allowed my mind to wander back to that last case. Maybe I had ruffled some feathers when working that case.

He was a defense contractor from Cocoa Beach. He was looking at a ton of taxes, not to mention civil fraud penalties. The criminal case had been dropped, so he wasn't faced with going to jail.

His case began with a referral from the office of U.S. Attorney Walther Roosevelt, who headed joint investigations between the Department of Justice (DOJ), IRS, FBI, and other government agencies united together in the war on terrorism. These joint investigations were centered around the idea that a paper trail could lead them to terrorist groups operating on U.S. soil. Referrals were generated by information or leads out of Mr. Roosevelt's office.

The IRS was following its roots by following the money trail. No different than what the IRS did with Al Capone a few decades back. What could not be accomplished by more traditional methods, such as waterboarding, was accomplished through IRS administrative actions.

No questions were asked of Mr. Roosevelt by the heads of the IRS on where he got the information that generated these referrals. Sometimes these leads snag individuals, like this defense contractor, who are not guilty of cavorting with terrorists, but just plain, old-fashioned tax fraud.

By the time his case made its way to my desk, he and his wife had divorced, and she had filed a claim for relief as an Innocent Spouse. She claimed she was an Innocent Spouse for tax purposes and should be granted relief and absolution of any taxes owed by her ex-husband. In her opinion, spending time in jail for tax fraud should not be in her cards.

Her only part in this matter was dutifully signing the joint tax return with her ex. I met with her high-powered tax attorney about her claim as an Innocent Spouse. When I told him, upon review, that she did not qualify as an Innocent Spouse because the facts suggested she knew all about the tax fraud, he turned to me and told me that the IRS was being used by the Department of Justice. That the fraud charges were all trumped up by someone high up in the Department of Justice.

Her costly attorney contended that her ex had been targeted for political reasons and that he was not the only one being harassed by the IRS. They had plans to go tabloid with the dirt if her case went to trial. Well, I had to give it to her and her tax attorney, leaping all the way back to the Nixon era to use the idea that the IRS was being used to audit folks for political reasons.

At the time, it seemed like a real stretch, but shortly after the case was settled before going to trial, my job was abolished, my office closed, and I was given my walking papers. I thought about what my mother had said earlier—I had ruffled some feathers.

Could those feathers have belonged to U.S. Attorney Walther Roosevelt? Nah, as usual, I dismissed her conjecture as the superstitious whims of a little old Greek lady who happened to be my mother. With no answers to the question, I finally dozed off.

As I look back on that night, I wish I had talked to her more about it and more important things between us because, as it was to turn out, it was one of our last conversations, at least on this earth.

CHAPTER 4

As I was having my morning coffee, I decided to call someone I knew at the Boca Vista sheriff's office. I wanted to see if I could learn more about Harry's death. Ernie had been less than forthcoming last night.

My connection, Rosie, was the dispatcher, so she knew pretty much what was going on at the sheriff's office. She also worked weekends at a bakery. Between the bakery and day old donuts at the sheriff's office, she had gained weight instead of losing it after her pregnancy. She recently joined me at Zumba.

From time to time I hired her to help out with filing since Velma despised doing it, and as a result, ignored filing around the office. Whenever our office started to look like we were hoarders, I called Rosie in to catch us up.

Velma is all of five foot four inches and quite voluptuous. She possesses a beautiful face with deep, dark eyes. Coincidentally, we both grew up in Fish Camp, and our paths seemed to crisscross during our working days with the IRS. Because I was also always on some new diet, she and I bonded through her battle to keep her weight under control. She blamed weight problem solidly on the men in her life and their preference for women with a little 'junk in the trunk' as she put it. "That's just the way it is with black men," she would tell me. "They prefer women with a little meat on their bones, not like white men who like their women all bone."

I had heard she decided not to accept any of the many lucrative government jobs she had been offered, and instead, she had also accepted the buyout.

She moved back to Fish Camp with her twin girls and in with her elderly mother. When I was setting up my tax office, I tracked her down, gave her a call and offered her a job. The next thing I knew, Velma was running my office, which suited me just fine.

"Rosie, it's me, MC. How's it going?"

"You must have ESP," Rosie said. "I just ate two jelly donuts."

"Rosie," I said, "you need to quit that bakery. It's like an alcoholic working in a bar."

"I know, I know," she said in her New England accent. Rosie had moved south from Boston to escape the cold. "I'm looking through the want ads as we speak."

"Look, that's not what I called about. Rosie, what can you tell me about a PI, Harry West? He was found shot dead."

"Oh yeah," she said. "It's all the talk here. In fact, the detectives in charge of the investigation are meeting with the feds right now about the case."

"Really?" I said. "FBI?"

"No, you would normally think that," Rosie said. "But, it's Homeland Security."

"Homeland Security," I said thinking to myself, 'Of course.' "Why is Homeland Security involved in this?"

"I'm not sure," Rosie said. "They seem to be keeping that part under wraps. It looked like a mugging gone badly at first, but I just heard today about the feds being in on the investigation. How come you're interested? Was he a client?"

"Something like that," I quickly said.

"Oh," Rosie said. "Well look, I can try to keep you in the loop if it helps."

"That would be great. Call me if you hear anything about what happened to him."

"I will," Rosie said. And then she added, "Right now they think it was a hit made to look like a mugging."

"Oh," I said.

"Yep," Rosie said.

"I heard that the bullet was point blank to the back of the head. He was probably forced to kneel and then poof, the lights went out."

"Wow," I said.

"I got to go, boss is coming my way," Rosie said. "I'll call you if I hear anymore." And she hung up the phone.

I stuck my cell in my purse and quickly got dressed to head into the office.

As I was driving, I was thinking about what Rosie had said: "A hit." Maybe Harry West was just looking into something going on with the grocery business. Maybe it had nothing to do with spooks; although, that would not explain why the feds were interested in the investigation.

The gossip column in the local Boca Vista newspaper reported that Babbs had talked Charlie into taking over the reins of the business after they married, and the rumor was that he had agreed, reluctantly. He had the skills and personality to run the business, and as her spouse, he was part of the family and spoke for her when it came to running the family grocery business.

This had allowed Babbs to return to her life as a social butterfly. All perfect, I surmised, until Charlie disappeared and Harry West, the PI, had wound up dead.

CHAPTER 5

I got into my office a little early still thinking about the conversation I'd just had with Rosie. Velma had not arrived yet, having to drop her two girls off at school. I wanted some time to think and get ready for the big meeting with Babbs at the mansion.

My tax and accounting office is in a storefront located on Worthy Row in Boca Vista, or Iguana Row as it's called by Fish Campers. It had once been a small boutique dress shop on a street lined with upscale, hoity-toity shops and restaurants that run parallel to a deep canal. My storefront location also boasted an office in the back with a window overlooking the canal and docks. The canal is lined with the mega-yachts of the mega-rich who couldn't find moorage in Fort Lauderdale or, for reasons of their own, prefer to hide out in Boca Vista.

The remodeled retail space up front contains Velma's command station with a couple of chairs and a coffee table with magazines for clients. Velma's desk area looks out a large front window on Iguana Row.

Velma seems to like the setup, too, watching all the traffic on the main drag and folks' reaction to the iguanas that populate the neighborhood, much to the dismay of the citizens of Boca Vista.

"Looky there," I'll hear Velma as she spots a visitor and watches their reaction to the iguanas. We have to watch the front door, so the iguanas don't meander in when a client arrives for an appointment. It's generally not a good first impression. An exception to that rule had been one iguana, in particular, Izzy, whom Velma had named and adopted.

Sipping my Cuban coffee, the caffeine was causing my eyes to dart around my office for signs of Izzy and his family when a loud bang at my back window catapulted me and my Cuban coffee right out of my chair.

I turned expecting to see a life-size Izzy, but instead, there stood Jennifer. "We need to talk," she mouthed like a mime. She was standing outside at the back window where Izzy had been the other day making goo-goo eyes at Babbs, and looking as if she just came from working out. She was wearing her sweats, and an 'I Love Nashville' ball cap over her Marilyn hair, which stuck out the back end, like a broom.

"Come around to the front," I mimed back while dabbing at the Cuban coffee, half of which had spilled on my white blouse and blue skirt. Great, this is no way to start the day, let alone go to my big meeting with Babbs at the mansion.

I let Jennifer in the front door, and she flew right by me into my office and sat down in the same spot she'd occupied the day before. She gave the chair a twirl and swung around to look at me as I sat down at my desk.

"I have some explaining to do, and I want you to listen before you jump to any conclusions," she said as I waited for the twirling in the chair to stop.

"Okay," I said.

"Charlie La-Fleur and I are not having an affair," she said somewhat exasperated while adjusting the Marilyn hair under the ball cap. "That woman is out of her mind."

"She won't even talk to me. Everything goes through Bruce for crying out loud! Like I said yesterday, Charlie La-Fleur is my CPA, period."

"Okay," I said and looked up to see Velma standing in the doorway.

"Good Morning, Velma," I said, thankful for the distraction. "You remember Ms. Stone."

"Yes, of course, I do," Velma said, and I could hear the silent "dummy."

"Good morning, Ms. Stone. Can I get you some coffee?" And, in the same breath, she said to me, "What happened to your blouse?"

"I had … a little accident," I said with a forced grin.

"Please, call me Jennifer. No coffee, but a bottle of water would be great, and thank you so much, Velma."

"No problem," Velma said as she went to get the water and shook her head at me.

Velma returned with the water and then sat down in

the seat next to Jennifer. Just like the other day, two women who were used to controlling the situation sitting across from my desk. I just gave Velma a look, and she looked back with a smile. Great! Next Izzy will pop in and hop up on my desk, and it will be a perfect morning.

Jennifer took a sip and then continued where she had left off. Velma and I gave her our undivided attention.

"Since Charlie was older than me, it was only natural that after a while he would take on a fatherly role, which was very comforting to me," she said.

"He would, though, ask my advice whenever he needed to buy a gift for Babbs. After all, the woman has everything, and you know how men are when they have to buy a gift for someone they care about. He truly loves her," Jennifer said looking at Velma for confirmation. *Yeah, and her money, too.*

Velma responded, "Of course."

We both looked at Velma for a second and then Jennifer continued.

"About two months ago, I was meeting with Charlie to go over my taxes when he asked me if I would mind keeping a package for him. He didn't say what it was, but I just assumed it was something for Babbs, and it was a surprise," Jennifer said.

"I said sure, no problem and the next day he

showed up at my house with the package. It was a large brown moving box. I thought it was a little strange at the time, but then I assumed he just had not gotten around to wrapping the present for Babbs," Jennifer said, tugging at her ball cap.

"He asked me to hold it for a few days, so we just stuck it in a safe place in my house, and that was the last I saw of Charlie. Frankly, I forgot all about it until Bruce contacted me asking about Charlie and where he was, as if I would know where he was, and all the while insinuating that I was having an affair with Charlie.

"Honestly, the guy is just so over the top and such a drama queen," Jennifer said. "I'm sure he went back to Babbs and stirred up the fire about an affair, and the next thing I knew we were all coming to your office for the meeting. Why would I know where he was?" She took a gulp of water.

"He is such a bitch," Velma said. I shot Velma a look like it's time to go up front now. She seemed to take the hint and got up.

"I think I hear the phone ringing," Velma said. "Nice to see you, Ms. Stone," she said as she made her exit.

I watched Velma leave and then gave Jennifer a quick smile and nod as if to say, "that Velma."

"So, you haven't seen Charlie since he dropped off the box?" I said to Jennifer who was now swooshing down the water.

She stopped and said, "That's right. Like I said, it was tax time. We were going over my taxes, and he was filing an extension for me."

I thought for a minute. "He was filing an extension so that would make it right before April 15?"

"Yes," Jennifer said. "I always wait until the last minute and usually drop by his office with my tax stuff right around April 15th. Charlie files the extension for me, and we file my taxes later. That's why I remember the date he dropped off the box. He said he was heading out for his fishing trip and would call me when he got back to finish my taxes and also pick up the box. That's the last I heard from Charlie."

We just sat there for a minute while I calculated the time that had passed. It was now the beginning of June, so Charlie had been missing for over a month if he took off right after April 15th.

As if she was reading my mind she said, "I still have the box."

"So, it's still in your house?"

"Yes," she said. "My house actually has some secret rooms my ex-husband, Harry Stone, had built into it," and she paused, "to store items."

The recent ex-husband being the alleged mafia lord/hedge fund manager, I thought.

"So, after I got the call from Bruce I remembered the box. That's where it is now," she said and finished the water.

"Does anyone else know about that room or the box?" I asked.

"No," Jennifer said. "The only one who knows about that room is my ex, and I don't think he'll be stopping by anytime soon. The last I heard he was out in Vegas. I haven't told anyone about the box. That's why I'm here, MC. I wanted to let you know I wasn't having an affair with Charlie, and I thought you should know about the box," Jennifer said.

I was thinking about this, and at the same time wondering if I could get a job back at the IRS.

"You haven't looked in the box, have you?" I asked.

Jennifer sat there for a minute, I could see there was a lot of thinking going on under the Marilyn hairdo, which was out from under the cap now. Processing, processing, geez these women, I thought.

"Well, I decided to check on it, and while I was checking on it, I did take a teeny peek in the box," Jennifer said.

"Oh, really," I said, and waited for the bomb to drop.

"What was in the box, Jennifer?" I said reluctantly. No turning back now; we were entering the Witch's Forest.

"A briefcase," Jennifer said, all the while watching

me for my reaction.

"A briefcase," I said, a little surprised now. These women, I thought staring at her. Dispensing information drip by drip like an IV stuck in your arm. She went on as if she was reading my mind.

"Yes, but it was locked," she said, and then she added, "I think there's cash in it."

She thinks there is cash in it, I thought. Of course, what else would be in it? It's probably a matching briefcase to go with a Prada purse.

"Why is that, Jennifer?" I asked as patiently as possible.

"Because I recognized the brand of the briefcase," she said.

Get to the point, please, I was thinking, and she did.

"Let's just say that my ex-husband brought home briefcases like it from time to time, if you get my drift."

If I got her drift, it was the Kmart blue light special, carry your cash in type of briefcase.

"Well, since you recognized the briefcase, and you know its use," I said. "Just how much cash would you estimate that briefcase is holding?"

Jennifer looked at me and said, "I really don't know, but I can tell you it's expandable and Charlie's briefcase was fully expanded."

Oh, I thought, it was the fully expandable cash

briefcase.

"Jennifer," I said falling back to my sternest IRS voice. "Listen very carefully because I am not going to repeat this twice. Does anyone else know about the briefcase?"

"No," she said, and I believed her, but then she was a good actress. "I haven't told a soul until now."

I let go of my breath. "Good. Let's keep it that way," I said.

"Well, except …" Jennifer said.

*Oh no, here it comes. I can hear the witch's monkeys on the way.*

"Except for your Aunt Sophia," she said in a whisper.

"My Aunt Sophia?" I cried.

"Why would you tell my Aunt Sophia anything, let alone about this briefcase," I asked in disbelief.

"Because your Aunt Sophia is my psychic. She knows everything anyway. It's in the cards," she said, and I think she added a silent "dummy."

"Oh, my lord," I just said, as I sat there in shock.

*Great, Aunt Sophia's involved. And where Aunt Sophia goes, Aunt Anna is not far behind.*

The phone buzzed, and I nearly jumped out of my chair. It was Velma.

"Have you forgotten about your appointment with Babbs?" she said.

I looked at my watch and saw I had just enough time to get over to the mansion.

"Jennifer," I said. "I have to go meet with Babbs now. Please, whatever you do, don't tell anyone else about this."

"Okay," she said and got up out of the chair to leave. Before she could say anymore, I said, "And that is all I am going to say on the matter until I've had a chance to sort this all out." She looked back at me as she headed out of my office. She seemed to be assimilating my message "All right," she said. "That's what Aunt Sophia told me to do before she told me to come over and talk to you."

*Good grief.* I watched her leave my office. The last thing I needed was my two aunts involved.

CHAPTER 6

While Velma and Jennifer were out front chatting it up, I dialed my aunts' telephone number hoping to catch them. But instead, I heard my Aunt Anna's voice on their voicemail, "If you're trying to reach Sophia or Anna, you're out of luck, so just leave a message and be quick about it, like a bunny." Great, I thought. I just hung up the phone and would deal with those two later. I had to get to the mansion for the big meeting with Babbs.

"Velma," I called from my office after Jennifer left. "You're going with me to this meeting. I think I'm going to need you there to help."

Velma came around the corner, purse in hand. "I'm ready," she said and handed me her office sweater, the one she kept draped over her chair for times when I turned the AC down due to hot flashes.

"What is this for?" I asked.

"What do you think?" Velma said and nodded toward the café au lait stain on my white blouse.

I grabbed the sweater out of her hands, and out the door, we went.

By the time we arrived at the La-Fleur mansion, I had filled Velma in on my meeting with Ernie at Hotel Florida and the rest of the conversation I'd just had with

Jennifer.

"Bruce said you should park around the side where the tour buses usually park, and come on in," Velma said. "He said the door would be open." As we got out of the car, Velma and I heard a car leaving. We both looked and saw Uncle Sal heading out.

We waved as he slowly went by and watched Uncle Sal wave back. We could see that he was steering his black Mercedes with his big old belly. We both watched as he swerved onto A1A and disappeared.

"That's as dangerous as texting and driving," Velma said.

I assumed she was thinking about her two girls who weren't old enough to drive, but Velma was a mother that started early.

"Did you have that talk with your twins?" I said.

"No, my Aunt Sadie."

"What?" I replied.

"Yep," she said, "Aunt Sadie."

Aunt Sadie was Velma's version of my Aunt Anna. Trouble spelled with a capital T. We headed toward the doors that led to the part of the mansion that was open for tours. This was the only part that I'd ever been through, having been dragged there by my mother who went on every possible tour while I was growing up and whenever extended family from Greece came to visit. It was called the "drive-by tour." Afterward, we would always stop for ice cream.

Actually, it was fascinating because it was a replica of the front of the mansion. From the parking lot, it looked as if they turned the house around and you were entering the front door of the mansion, just like a normal guest.

It sort of reminded me of Graceland because, as you stepped past the two white columns and into the mansion, you entered a living room and foyer just like Graceland. I wondered if we were going to catch a glimpse of the King today.

When Velma and I entered, I looked around expecting Bruce to greet us, but instead, a young man dressed in an expensive Italian suit entered the foyer. He immediately smiled and offered us his hand.

"Ms. Mahoney," he said. "Welcome to the mansion."

"Thank you," I said, and as I returned the handshake, I could see a holster and small gun strapped to his midsection. His eyes dropped down to my blouse and the coffee stain, which the sweater didn't entirely hide.

"This is, Velma, she will be assisting me," I said hoping to distract him while I buttoned up the sweater.

As he shook Velma's hand, she piped up as she nodded her head, "That's a nice little Berretta you have there."

I turned to look at Velma with my "are you out of your mind" smile as I finished buttoning the top of the sweater and watched as he held her gaze and handshake a little longer.

"Nice to meet you," he said, as he ignored Velma's comment.

Neither Velma nor I were surprised to pick up the sound of a slight Brooklyn accent, or that he looked the part of one of Jennifer's husbands. He was young, in his late twenties, tall, dark, and handsome, with the expensive suit, loafers, matching gun and holster.

He introduced himself. "I am Dominic Napolitano, and I moved down recently to help my father Sal with the family business," he said, his dark eyes not matching the smile on his good-looking face.

Hmm, I thought, and both Velma and I gave each other a quick glance. The town had heard about Dominic, Sal's only child, and his move back to Boca Vista recently, out of the blue, to help his father.

 He really was Babbs's cousin and young enough to be her grandson, which is probably why he addressed the Queen as Aunt Babbs. The rumor was that he was here for the money.

After his introduction, he turned and walked to a small door, which looked like a hall closet. When he opened the door, it revealed a long hallway, which was an entrance to the private part of the mansion.

"Won't you please come this way?" he asked and pointed us both through the doorway.

"My aunt will be with you shortly, but she asked that I greet you and show you to your office, which will be available to you while you are working here, at the mansion."

With that, he turned on his snazzy heels, and we followed him down the hallway and entered through a secure door into the main house. The house was ornately decorated. I felt as if I was walking through one of the old Florida baronial mansions. It reminded me of a house I had seen in Palm Beach. Large, twenty-foot windows opened to a spectacular view of the beach.

Velma and I continued to follow Dominic, taking it all in, until we arrived at a room about the size of a small house. The room, like the rest of the house, opened to a view of the ocean that was only broken by the clouds and a sailboat a long way off on the horizon.

In the middle of the room I saw a large desk with computers and several chairs, and off to the side a living and small dining room arrangement. It was furnished with mansions-to-go furniture. Then, on a large conference table, which extended the length of the room, both Velma and I saw the boxes at about the same time. I heard her mumble under her breath, "I see dead people."

There were more boxes than I had seen since my

days with the IRS. I assumed the boxes contained the records I was hired to go through to locate Charlie. It was a good thing I'd brought Velma because Babbs was not kidding when she had said at our meeting that I would have access to all her records.

Dominic gave us a minute to take in the boxes and then said, "This will be your office. Please make yourselves at home. On the wall is an intercom system. Anytime you need anything, please use it, and someone will tend to your needs immediately."

"Where is the ladies room?" Velma asked as once again I gave her the "what the heck" smile.

Dominic looked at her for a moment and then said to me, "Right over there." He pointed to a door in the corner and lifted his arm, so Velma and I got another view of the pistol and the holster attached to what I imagined were some well-defined pectoral muscles.

"Aunt Babbs will be here in a few minutes," he said.

He pointed to another corner of the room and said, "Over there you'll find a pot of freshly brewed coffee and fruit." And then he looked at Velma and added, "And some Danishes."

We both looked at what appeared to be a small kitchen in another part of the room and could see the goodies sitting piled on a granite counter right next to a microwave oven and a small refrigerator.

"Food, I'm starved," Velma said, and we both watched as Velma headed toward the Danishes.

"My goodness, would you look at this," she said, as she picked up a Danish from the middle of the tray.

She then walked over and stood directly in front of Dominic and said, while she bit off half of it. "My favorite, cheesecake, you shouldn't have," she said as she finished it.

"It was very nice meeting you," Dominic said, as we watched Velma walk over to the table and bite into another Danish. "I hope you are able to locate Charlie and he is safe. It is of grave concern to my Aunt Babbs."

"I will do my best," I said, as I looked into his empty eyes. With that, he left the room.

I walked over and poured myself a cup of coffee, and since I was hungry grabbed a Danish. It's in my genes, and I needed a little sugar in the bloodstream.

Velma was now inspecting the boxes. I walked over to join her, and we both stood there staring at the table piled with boxes.

"I don't like him," Velma said.

"Gee, Velma," I said. "I sort of gathered that. Try to remember these are our clients. We're not working for the IRS anymore."

I don't think she heard me because she replied, "I also think you might consider asking the Queen for more money."

"Velma," I said as I tried to snatch the remainder of her third Danish out of her hand, "be nice. I have no intention of asking for more money," I said. "I'd have to get a bigger safe deposit box. I just want to get in here and get out with a good enough lead to turn over to Queen Babbs, and she can take it from there if by that time Charlie hasn't dragged his sorry ass back home."

"From the sounds of your meeting with Ernie, I would say that's not going to happen anytime soon," Velma said, eyeing another tray piled high with finger food.

"He's got you on this case for his reasons, and it involves more than finding Charlie. He wants to know what happened to the PI, Harry West. I'm not sure what it is, but from the looks of all this Babbs and Ernie are both looking for Charlie, but for very different reasons."

She took one more look at the mountain of boxes and said, as she walked back and forth between the Danish and the finger food, "I think we're going to need help."

I took another look at the boxes and decided I needed another Danish.

As Velma and I sat there on the sofa making ourselves at home in the mansion, drinking coffee and eating little finger sandwiches, I began to wonder how I could approach Dominic for a workout area for our quarters. In mid-thought, Queen Babbs slipped into the room. I immediately straightened up and placed the china coffee cup on the table spilling a little of its contents on the parquet floor. You would think I was back at St. Mary's parochial grade school and Sister Scalda, the most feared nun by all, had just entered the room.

Babbs caught the spill as I quickly dabbed it with a napkin and she said, "Relax, I want you to be comfortable while you are here."

Velma, surprisingly, straightened up, too, and placed her sandwich and napkin on the coffee table in front of us.

Babbs was dressed in the uniform of the very wealthy. It was a casual but elegant outfit, her hair was pulled back, her makeup flawless, and the whole look was comfortably rich. White slacks and sandals, black knit top, gold earrings, gold necklace and gold Rolex.

Babbs's maiden name was Napolitano. Her father was Dominic, and her Uncle Sal was her father's younger brother. The richest family in Boca Vista, they had the privilege of running the joint.

Velma had filled me in on some family history on the ride over. I got most of the inside scoop from Velma, who seemed to know everything going on around town, just like she did at the IRS.

Babbs's father, Dominic, had moved to Boca Vista from Chicago and told the town that he owned a grocery business in Chicago.

"Dominic soon became the town's biggest benefactor. The town leaders liked his plan to establish Boca Vista as a swanky Palm Beach type tourist stop along A1A.

When Babbs was ten years old, her mother died suddenly. Not long after that her father, Dominic, was whacked gangland style. Sal, Dominic's younger brother, and his wife Stella came from Chicago, to take Babbs with them, back to Chicago.

The town leaders of Boca Vista began to wonder what was going to happen to their community if the family took Babbs and went back to Chicago along with all that money.

The town set out to do something to save the golden goose and approached Sal with an offer, a tract of land with a new office building for the headquarters of the family grocery business.

It was an offer Sal could not refuse since he was faced with raising his brother's only child and heading the family business. His wife, Stella, also liked the idea of moving to sunny Florida since she had relatives in Miami. So he accepted the town's offer, and he and his wife Stella moved the family grocery business to Boca Vista, and they moved into the mansion to care for Babbs. Soon they became the new royal family of Boca Vista and were quite content in that role.

The younger Dominic, who we just met, was the

product of Sal's marriage to a trophy wife Sal had made the mistake of marrying out of grief, right after his wife, Stella, had died. She took off with a ton of money in a divorce after she produced his son, Dominic. They hadn't seen her since.

Dominic worked in the casino business in New Jersey. He had shown up conveniently one day, just about the time his father's health was failing. Taking a break from his jet set lifestyle to attend to his father and/or muscle his way into the family fortune.

Babbs went over to the coffee pot and poured herself a cup of coffee, but both Velma and I noticed she passed on the Danish, probably how she stayed so pencil thin. She came over and sat down in a chair, on the other side of the sofa, across from Velma.

We both waited for Babbs to open the conversation, after all, she was royalty.

"I really didn't mean to be so hard on Jennifer the other day in your office. I am just so distraught over not hearing from Charlie," Babbs said, as she sipped her coffee out of the china cup she held gracefully in her manicured hands. *Oh, brother, back to the soap opera.*

I really didn't know how to respond to this, so I kept my mouth shut, which was hard to do since she was trying to draw me into a conversation, just like two old friends. Velma was also quiet, which was really strange.

"Being somewhat older than Charlie, I tend to be

insecure where he is concerned, especially with someone as young and beautiful as Jennifer. I've since had a chat with Bruce, and yes, he does tend to exaggerate," she said, as she took another sip of coffee.

*Exaggerate? The guy's a walking poster child for a drama queen.*

Her facial expression changed quickly from the girlfriend chit chat to all business, "I am telling you this to let you know what type of man Charlie was and hoped that I didn't lead you astray with my feelings toward Jennifer."

"No, not at all," I heard myself saying. "I appreciate your frankness."

"My hope is that he will show up in the next few days and put an end to this mystery," Babbs said. "But, I fear that may not happen. Harry West, the private investigator, had been hired for another matter. Later, I asked him to find Charlie. Now, he is dead and, I fear, murdered. I want you to search these books and records. If something bad has happened to Charlie, I want you to find out," and then she added in almost a whisper, "even if it points to a member of my family."

This took me a little by surprise, so I just sat there for a minute, processing, processing.

"I really don't know what to say, if you think something like that has happened to Charlie then I must advise you to contact the police," I said.

"No," she said firmly, and I felt my back stiffen up like I did in grade school back at St. Mary's. Where was Velma's big mouth when I needed some input? I glanced over at Velma, and she was just sitting there taking this all in.

"I hired you to find him, and I am confident that you and maybe only you have the skills to find Charlie," Babbs went on. "After that, I will take care of the matter."

*Oh boy, she will take care of the matter? Was she nuts? Who was she going to take care of this matter with? Not Bruce the Queen Bitch?* I felt my palms getting a little sweaty as I carefully took another sip of coffee and looked sideways at Velma. Still stone-faced, that Velma. *Where is that scoundrel Charlie?*

"There is also a matter of something Charlie may have been holding for someone, for safekeeping . When you find it, I want you to tell me, and then I will handle the retrieval."

*When I find it? Now what? Retrieval? Will I need a hazmat suit?* Velma was now awakening from her trance and shot me a quick glance as we watched Babbs get up to pour herself another cup of coffee.

I was sure we were both thinking the same thing. Did Babbs know about the briefcase/cash Charlie had given to Jennifer to sit on? Did I miss something here? Was the Queen being selective about the questions she chose to answer, but you must obey her commands just the same?

Babbs returned and sat her coffee down. Her expression changed again to one of a friend. "You will know what it is—if and when you find it," she said.

"Let's just say, MC," and she now was leaning close to me and patting my arm, "you were trained all your life to recognize this," and then she smiled, Queenly.

"We will cross that bridge when we come to it, but for now, let's go over the records so you can get started. I would like regular reports on your progress. You will report to me and no one else. My Uncle Sal is not well, and his son, Dominic, whom you just met, I will take care of keeping him apprised, of course."

*Yeah sure. Great.* I was really feeling like I was wading into some deep water here, but it also seemed as if I had no choice but to plunge in and see if I could find out what happened to Charlie. The fact that my mother decided I should not learn how to swim when I was a kid because she was afraid I would drown was not helping me now.

At some point, I would have to decide what to do. I really didn't like getting this close to the Napolitano family. I wouldn't be surprised if the family and Jennifer's exes were investors in the same joint ventures.

Babbs escorted Velma and me to the conference table, and we spent the rest of the meeting going over the boxes and the records.

Basically, the boxes held tax returns organized by year, as well as books and records and bank records and credit card records. These were financial records that left a trail of money spent, and where, over a period of time. Once organized chronologically, it would be just a matter of following the trail. Hopefully, it would take us to that scoundrel, Charlie.

Babbs then showed us the computerized records, and we spent the next half hour getting me up to speed on the computerized accounts. Babbs then left us alone to do a little work and gave us instructions on how to access the office each time we came to the mansion, so we could come and go as necessary.

After she had left, I decided to call Ernie on my cell to bring him up to speed. I told him that Velma and I had just had our first meeting with Babbs.

He said we should meet tomorrow at my office to check in but to get as much done today with the records to see if we saw a trail that could point us quickly to Charlie. I decided to hold off on telling him about the cash and Jennifer, at least for now.

Velma and I grabbed a few more sandwiches and decided to put the boxes in categories. On one table, we placed Charlie's business records, which we divided up between tax returns, bank and credit card statements and a printout of his accounting books and records.

On the other table, we placed the personal records

of Babbs and Charlie and divided them up likewise: joint tax returns, bank and credit card statements. We also had a printout of their personal books and records.

We then decided to start by going over the printout of Charlie's books and the printout of their personal books. By the time we were finished, Velma and I concluded that, for the most part, it was pretty cut-and-dried and did not see anything unusual.

It was getting late, so we decided to start with the bank and credit card statements on our next visit and made our way out of the mansion to drive back to the office. The most recent credit card statements most likely would give us the trail to find Charlie. Going through all the other records was just a matter of making sure we knew what we were given and/or not given.

Velma grabbed her luggage size purse and walked over to the food table and picked up dinner for a family of ten from the remaining sandwiches and fruit. I just stood there and stared at her.

"Why not?" she said. "It will just go to waste."

She must have been channeling my mother because when she said that, just for a moment, I thought I heard my mother's voice.

I looked at her, rolled my eyes and then walked over and grabbed my own to-go box.

On the drive out, we passed Uncle Sal who was

belly driving and swerving his way back toward the mansion. I looked over at Velma who was now taking a little nap and decided I was going to talk to Little Dominic about adding a gym to our office space.

Izzy was waiting for us at the door. "You know, Velma," I said as she unlocked the door to the office, "we really have to do something about Izzy." She ignored me, and as I followed Velma into the office. Izzy slid in heading over to his perch.

"Remember I told you that Ernie was a spook, a big-time spook," Velma said as she followed me and watched me collapse into the chair in my office.

"I know, but since it looks like he got me into this mess in the first place, I'll just have to deal with it. It's not like we are still working for the IRS and have the power of all that bureaucracy behind us."

She thought about that for a moment, dropped the subject, and went back up front to her command station.

"I don't think hooking up with Ernie is such a good idea," I heard her say, "but, you're the boss."

Then she added, "If you keep him out of the picture, it's just a classic investigative accounting case, but with Ernie, you are adding another dimension of strange. Like the Twilight Zone." Velma was a fan of old TV shows and movies.

"Yeah, well, until you have a better idea as to how to get out of this mess without Ernie, I'll just have to play it by ear," I said.

Velma came back into the office and looked as if she was going to reveal something, but then changed her mind and went back out to her station.

*OK, be that way.* I relied on Velma's common sense, but I was getting more worried by the minute. When we left the mansion, I noticed that a black Mercedes followed us all the way back to the office, that was the car of choice for the Napolitano family.

As we got out of my car when we reached the office, I could have sworn it was Dominic I saw driving as it quickly drove by. What was up with that? I put that out of my mind and got back on the phone attempting to get a hold of my two aunts, but still getting their annoying voice mail. Now there was another dimension.

## CHAPTER 7

It had been a long day, and soon after we got back to the office from our big meeting with Queen Babbs, it was time for Velma to leave to pick up her two girls and begin the second part of her work day. I decided to head home and track down my two aunts to make sure they did not become any more involved, other than Aunt Sophia advising Jennifer through her fortune-telling cards.

I had a key to their condo, so after I rang the bell and knocked, I used it and opened the door expecting to see the two of them sitting around my mom's dining room table. When I cashed in my buyout I utilized some of it to open the small tax office in Boca Vista, and, reluctantly, made use of most of the rest to make a down payment on a small condo in the same condominium complex as my mother and aunts, but one building away from them.

When I walked into their condo, I could see they were not home. I walked up to the table and placed my hand on the chair at the head of the table where my mother had sat and was left that way by my aunts.

"Ok, Mom," I heard myself saying out loud. "I need to talk to your two sisters, and I need to talk to them now."

My mother had two priorities in her life, which kept

it simple and easy to stay focused. Family first, and after that, she wanted to be in show business and become a star.

Whether it was as a singer in the big bands when she was younger or in the movies, TV, whatever; she just wanted to be a star. Someone you would recognize on the street and ask for an autograph. When Fish Camp acquired a public access TV studio, my mother was there knocking on the door as soon as it opened. Shortly afterward, she became a TV producer and brought her two sisters and anyone else she could grab along for the ride. That kept her going until she left this earth to cross the shore.

"In life, the balance sheet does not always balance," was her usual response to my attempts to get her to balance her checkbook and not spend cash on birthday cakes for everyone she knew who was having a birthday. Any excuse for cake and ice cream. "I need the sugar," she would say when I would argue, in vain, with her about her weight and health.

Or, "Never forget asses on a balance sheet come in all sizes," she would say with her Greek accent, and then the dark eyes would peer down her distinctive Greek nose at me. "Mom," I would say, "Its assets not asses."

"Whatever," she would shout back. "You get the message." Yes, when it came to my mother we always got the message.

I nearly jumped when I heard the front door open behind me, and there they were, my aunts Sophia and Anna. Aunt Sophia was the taller of the two. Aunt Anna did not get the height when it was passed out the day she was born, she was up to no good even on that day.

"Ahh, good you're here," my Aunt Anna said. "Sit down, we'll bring some food, and then we will look at the cards. We think we have a lead on Jennifer's friend, Charlie."

My Aunt Sophia and I just stood there looking at Aunt Anna. The evil eye was on my Aunt Sophia's face. "Anna," she said, "put a lid on it and follow me into the kitchen."

"You too," she said to me as she led the way to the kitchen.

"What? What?" Aunt Anna said.

"You know what!" Aunt Sophia replied. What happened next was a five-minute argument half in Greek and half in English, the gist of which was a reminder to Aunt Anna to not disclose what went on during the card readings.

It was a violation of the fortune teller card reading code. I decided to leave the two of them to hash it out, and went back into their living room and wait for the food, which came out right after the shouting stopped.

After a little spanakopita and Greek wine, it was just us around the table: Sophia, Anna, and me, and, in spirit, my mother.

Aunt Sophia spoke first and, as usual, got right to the point. "I was reading the cards, and I saw a very black cloud over your head. What are you getting yourself into? Are you not eating? I will bake some moussaka for you tomorrow. Put a little meat on those bones." Moussaka is a baked dish with eggplant, potatoes, onions, ground beef, milk, and butter. It is guaranteed to put a little meat on your bones. Food: the solution and the problem.

It was incredible to me how much Aunt Sophia sounded like my mother at times. It was as if Aunt Sophia was channeling a message from my mother.

I looked at Aunt Sophia, rolled my eyes, let out a big sigh, and walked into the kitchen to pour myself another glass of Greek wine since I didn't have far to drive, to the elevator and then a short walk to the safety of my condo. The kitchen of Aunt Sophia and Aunt Anna was always calling my name; my aunts usually cooked enough food for a Greek restaurant.

As I turned to head back into the meeting room, there was Aunt Anna.

"Well. You heard Sophia. She has seen it in the cards. What are you up to?" Aunt Anna had placed herself squarely in front of me. Aunt Anna was about five inches shorter than me, and, at times like this, I felt like I was looking down at one of the munchkins from *The Wizard of Oz*.

The next thing I knew Aunt Sophia was in the kitchen, and so I decided to lead the two of them back to the dining room table for a little family pow-wow.

It was a special table, which they had inherited from my mom, and I suppose one day will become mine. The table had originally belonged to my grandmother.

It was solid oak and ornate with four pedestal feet in the center, holding the table down like an anchor. Every time I saw it I remembered being a kid and crawling through those four pedestal feet.

The table was the center of many family feasts, holidays, funerals, and meetings. The oak in that table held the remnants of conversations long over, but at times the echo of those conversations could be heard.

It also was the office for my two aunts and their fortune-telling business. My aunts and my mother possess strands of psychic DNA. Apparently, I do too, but I'm not ready to go there. I knew not to bother them if the 'do not disturb' sign was on their front door. That meant business hours were in session.

I spoke first, "We need to have a family meeting, and the two of you need to hear exactly what I have to say to you," for a change, I thought, as I scooted the two of them back to the family dining room table and we took our seats.

Not wasting any time, I began, "now, I don't know what you two have seen in that deck of cards, but you need to keep it between the two of you. And, you both need to keep out of *it* and please do not dispense any more fortune-telling advice to Jennifer Stone dealing with *it.*"

I could tell by the looks on their faces that they knew what *it* was; *it* meaning finding Charlie must have come up in the conversation with Jennifer during her card reading.

"Do you hear me?" I said as if talking to two children.

"Fine," they both said at the same time.

Fine. I knew what 'fine' meant, and it wasn't the response I was looking for. With those two it usually meant, 'I hear you, but I may or may not agree' and if the 'fine' came along with a little tone it meant 'I will do what I darn well please.'

"You know, you might want to find a way to spend a little time with Jennifer," Aunt Anna said. "Bruce says she has a way with men, and you might learn a few tricks from her." With that, she winked her eye.

Oh, for crying out loud, there it was. She had an opportunity for a message, and Aunt Anna took it and conveniently turned the table around on me.

Well, I wasn't going to let her win the power play tonight. We will cover my disastrous love life some other night. It would take a lot more wine for that discussion.

"The only tricks I want to learn from her are how to

keep you two out of harm's way. This is serious business, and I want you both to keep your Greek noses out of it."

"Fine," they both said, and then the bobbleheads nodded in unison.

Oh, forget it, I thought. I'll work on them later. I was tired. The wine and food were putting me to sleep.

"Look, I'm going home to bed. You two need to think about what I said. It's not a TV show. It's real."

More bobbleheads. Fine. Fine and dandy. I left the two of them watching old reruns of Carson.

I dragged my tail home and plopped into bed.

In the middle of the night, the light went on. It was about the time my mother crossed the shore that the lamp on my nightstand would flicker on in the middle of the night. I kept my mother's prayer books, bibles and rosaries stuffed in the top drawer of that nightstand. When I mentioned it to my Aunt Sophia, she said "It's your mother. She's letting us all know that she may be across the shore, but she is still the boss and is watching over us."

I turned it off, and it went on again. This went on for a while until I unplugged the lamp and then slept like a baby. *Fine, just fine.*

CHAPTER 8

From afar, Ernie was slender with his white hair pulled back in a ponytail, usually wearing jeans and cowboy boots. Without a doubt, he caught your eye, but he still was able to blend in just like a chameleon.

He also walked with a slight limp some days, a result of a job-related injury. He never explained how that went down, but I had heard from a few of his patrons at the tiki bar that it had to do with a mission protecting the president while on loan to the Secret Service.

Ernie was sitting in my office when I got in the next morning. Velma had let him in and was up front on the phone as I came in the door. She placed her hand over the phone and said, "The spook is in there waiting for you."

"Who?"

"The spook," she said with a nod of her head toward my office, and then she went back to her phone conversation.

As I entered my office and before I could say hello, Ernie said, "Sit down, we need to talk, and you need to listen before you say anything."

"Fine," I heard myself say as I sat down and looked across my desk at Ernie who was sitting in the queen chair. This desk was starting to remind me of my mother's dining room table. What's next, fortune-telling cards would appear in the middle of the desk? Ernie tended to be direct and to the point.

I folded my arms in front of me and said, "Okay Ernie, I'm listening, but I want to hear the whole story. And please, along the way, tell me why you've got me spearheading this hunt for Charlie because I know you were the one who pointed Babbs and her new best bud, Jennifer, in my direction. From what I'm learning, it's more of a job for you or someone in their *grocery business*."

"No MC, that's where you are wrong. It's a job tailor-made for you," and then I thought I could hear a door creaking open. "Although, it did start with Charlie and the *grocery business*."

Ernie gave me a long, hard stare. No doubt he'd taken down a few bad guys with that stare. But, I wasn't going down that easy. "MC, I sent Babbs to you because you are the best one for this job. Believe it or not, your unique IRS skills are far more suited to finding Charlie or discovering what happened to him than anyone else. And, to be fair, you need to know a little about more about the Napolitano family and their *grocery business*."

"Fine," I said. "I'm all *ears*." He gave me the stare down and then I heard the door open. I was quiet and still.

"Babbs's father, Dominic, really was in the grocery

business, but the business was also a front for his main operation, which was laundering money for the mob. Dominic, like you, was a pro with numbers and accounts and soon moved up the ranks of the mob hierarchy by becoming the laundry man. He ran it through his grocery business.

I remained quiet and still while he continued.

"In recent years, Sal has shifted the grocery business in a more legitimate direction.

"You may also know that, Sal's son, Dominic, has shown up in town," Ernie added with a slight hint of a sneer, I thought.

As I sat there and took this all in, I could only think about Velma's warning. I should have listened to her from day one; she tried to warn me about the Napolitano family and she sure as heck was never a fan of Ernie and all of his spook friends.

"Charlie La-Fleur took over as chief financial officer for Babbs's family after they married, along with continuing to run his CPA firm in Boca Vista. He is also the CPA for Boris Rusky," Ernie said.

"Boris and Natasha?" I said.

I knew Boris and his wife, Natasha, and had seen their son Joe over the years. Who could miss him? Like Jennifer, he turned heads with his good looks. They were the Fish Camp counterparts of the Napolitano family.

They kept a lower profile and operated a string of gasoline stations throughout Florida. They owned all the honky-tonk bars in town and had a row of them in downtown Fish Camp just like Nashville. Joe was another one that Jennifer had under her spell. Only he was a little proactive. He would love for Jennifer to settle down with him and start making bambinos. Jennifer, of course, was not ready, still looking for her star in Hollywood.

"Wait a minute. Are you going to tell me that their business is a front for the mob?" I heard myself out of the blue say to Ernie.

Ernie gave me his famous stare, and I knew the answer–maybe–maybe not.

"MC, you are working on a matter that involves more than just a wife trying to locate her bad boy husband who has been missing for a couple of weeks. It's a matter that has to do with national security, and let's just say I have been *reactivated* to look into the matter."

I sat there dumbfounded. Maybe Aunt Sophia was right about that black cloud!

"What?" I said. "Wait, if you have been *reactivated*, then does this have something to do with terrorism?" I must have stumbled into that psychic room I usually avoid. With that, he got up and began to leave. As he got near the door to my office, he turned to me and said, "Look, MC. I have told you all you need to know for now, and any more would place you in harm's way. Keep looking through the books and records and tracking down all leads to find out what happened to Charlie." Then he added a twist. "It's possible that somewhere in the records Babbs gave you, you will find a second set of books," he said.

My head was spinning. So that's what Queen Babbs meant during our meeting at the mansion when she said I would know it when I saw it having been trained all my life for this.

"Ernie, wait a minute. I'm just an accountant, a former government employee of the IRS, for heaven's sake, not a spook. I don't even own a gun."

"Leave the guns to me, but, as a precaution, I am sending someone over to train you and Velma in firearms," he said.

"Velma?" I said.

"Yes, she is part of the team. I spoke to her before you got to the office this morning. Velma actually is very handy with a gun."

"She is? Who are you sending?"

"Rodeo," he said.

Of course, I thought, Velma won't like this, but apparently, he convinced her to join the team, or maybe she was already part of this team?

Then he turned to leave, but looked back at me and said, "MC, I wouldn't have gotten you involved in this assignment if I didn't know you could handle it. The fact of the matter is you were well known in certain IRS circles as the best when it came to following a paper trail. Just use your investigative accounting ability to hunt down Charlie, and I'm hoping it will also lead to an answer to what happened to that PI, Harry West."

I remembered what Rosie had told me and shot back, "Is that why the Feds are talking to the local sheriff? Was Harry West *reactivated* like you?"

He turned and walked back into my office, placed his hands on my desk, leaned over and spoke directly to me in a whisper and said, "Yes."

As I held my breath, he placed his trump card in the middle of my desk, so to speak. To make sure I was hooked just like those two women the other day. Only it wasn't cash, it was information.

"By the way, you've stepped on some big toes. That's why your job at the IRS was axed. We'll talk about that another day. I promise you."

With that, he headed out of my office, "TMI," I thought. As I sat there not moving and just thinking while my brain went over the conversation I'd just had with Ernie, the spooky bartender.

His last words about stepping on some big toes left me curious. Did he know whose toes I stepped on and why I was pushed out the door? He knew I would follow his lead now, just to find out what he was talking about and the promise he made to reveal that mystery someday.

Later that evening I went for a long run. For a control freak, it always surprised me that I never was really in control of my life. Maybe it was time to move on to another line of work. Heading back to my condo, I looked up at my aunts' windows and could see the lights were on. Right now, reading the family fortune-telling cards like my mother and aunts was looking pretty good.

CHAPTER 9

Investigative accountants are the Aunt Sophia's of the accounting world. They are not reading cards, but instead, are reading the books and records of an accounting system. They look for evidence of natural and not so natural phenomena in the books and records.

I was sitting in my office the next day thinking that Ernie was right. I was trained to be a specialist in that field by the IRS. We had been given broad powers to investigate white-collar crime. We tracked down money launderers, drug dealers, and high-profile criminals through a thorough analysis of their books and records, which could possibly hold the clues to what they may not have reported on their tax returns. After 9/11, the focus moved from the mob to terrorists.

I knew that men like Ernie were integral to our investigations. They obtained crucial information through covert operations. I never went out in the field and never had to go to court to testify. I was the ghost in the machine, and that suited me just fine. As the memory of 9/11 began to fade in the minds of the country, so did the emphasis on finding terrorists.

I now thought of my mother's words: *You must have ruffled some feathers.* Once again, as I look back on our conversations, she was right.

"Are you listening to me?" I heard Velma say. "I told you not to get involved with that spook."

I was sitting in the office with Velma bringing her up to speed on my meeting the day before with Ernie.

"Velma," I said, "He showed up and made himself right at home."

"I don't like this any more than you do, and as soon as I can find a way for the both of us to get out of this spider's web, we will. But for now, it looks like we are both stuck," I said. At least until we can locate that jerk, Charlie, I thought to myself.

"You know what I think?"

I looked at Velma's eyes for a clue.

"Somehow Charlie's disappearance is tied into this bigger thing that Ernie is involved in, but I think there's more to it than he has told us. I think something else is in all those books and records, and that's what he wants you to find."

"Yes," I said. "I think you are right and I also think that bigger thing is to find out what happened to his friend, the PI, Harry West. It's all tied into this mess, and I think that's the real reason Ernie has gotten involved. There is always an emotional link."

Velma just looked at me thinking about something. "I work for you and will back you up, but remember, I'm no longer working for Uncle Sam and don't have to go down that road anymore," she said.

"Well, unfortunately, I think we both have been drafted." Waiting for the right moment, I added, "By the way, Ernie told me that I did step on someone's toes and those toes were in some big shoes, which led to my job being axed."

"Did he say who?" she asked.

"No, he didn't say," I replied. "He dangled that as a carrot to keep me following his orders. But I thought maybe you could shed some light on that shadow?"

With that Velma gave me a long stare and then said, "I might." But before she could say any more, we heard someone open the front door. She got up and just stood still by my office door.

Her expression changed immediately to one of her 'if looks could kill' stares. She watched as someone entered the front door to the office, and I knew instinctively that someone was Rodeo.

"Hello, good-looking," I could hear him say to Velma.

Rodeo was another former Homeland Security, prior military, Special Ops, Navy Seal type who I suspected worked with Ernie in the *field*. Velma knew him. His story was a lot like Ernie's. He had taken early retirement from Homeland Security. But, Velma suspected that he had branched out on his own as a freelance operative, jack-of-all-trades type.

From time to time, he showed up at Ernie's tiki bar, and rumor was that he lived in Fort Lauderdale. I had no idea what his real name was, but I had a sneaky suspicion Velma did. To say he was good-looking was a gross understatement.

He stood over six feet tall and could easily be mistaken for an NFL player. His skin was a warm cocoa shade, and his face was chiseled like a statue. When he walked, every woman within five feet stopped and took notice, especially of his gluteus maximus, or tush, in plain English.

Velma stood mesmerized by Rodeo when he entered the office. I always thought, by the way she spoke of him when his name came up in conversation, that they had some connection. Velma had confided in me once that she had met Rodeo years ago when she was younger and much slimmer. I could tell by the look in both of their eyes now that maybe my thoughts on that matter were true.

"Hello good-looking?"

"Don't you hello good-looking me," Velma said.

Oh boy, this wasn't looking good.

Rodeo walked up to Velma and whispered something in her ear while looking my way with a quick wink.

I could tell she was taken, and actually, so was I.

"Humph," I heard from Velma.

Velma walked into the center of my office and pointed at Rodeo while she said, "Well, you see who's here. Ernie has sent his partner in crime. You and I are in some deep crap."

Rodeo strolled into my office, and he pulled out the chair for Velma, who sat down without looking at him. He then pulled the other chair back and sat down, so he could look at the both of us.

"You're looking good, Miss MC."

"Thank you Rodeo, you look as good, also, as usual," I said, not thinking just looking, tongue-tied around the shoelaces to my shoe, which I had just placed in my mouth. Again.

I couldn't believe I'd said that, and Velma was looking at me as if I was nuts.

"Ernie sent me over to give you both some firearms training. I already know Velma can handle a gun pretty well, how about you MC?"

"I never touch the stuff," I said.

"That's what I thought," he said, as he looked directly at me. "I will make arrangements to pick you both up and go to the range," he said still looking at me.

"But MC, before I do that I wanted to stop by and give you your first lesson on handling a gun." He paused and then said, "Lesson number one is that you have to pull the trigger. Because if you don't pull the trigger, there is no reason for lesson number two." I sat there thinking about what he had just said.

"Now I know Ms. Velma can pull the trigger," Rodeo said as if speaking from memory.

Velma looked at Rodeo like she was about to pull the trigger.

"But I'm not so sure about you, MC."

"Rodeo, come on, I'm an accountant, not a cop or military."

"Well, my job is going to be to get you to where you have that cop mentality because you may need to pull that trigger to save your life," and then he looked in Velma's direction, "or someone else's."

With that, I just sat in my chair and ran my fingers up and down my forehead. I really didn't need this, but I also knew Rodeo was dead serious. He seemed to take that as a cue to make his exit.

"I'll call Velma. Pack a light bag. The training is not going to be in little Palm Beach," he said as he got ready to leave.

"What?" I said.

"We will be flying you both to Quantico for the training."

"What?" I said again. "We can't just go down to the firing range in Fish Camp?"

"No," he said, still looking at me. I felt a trickle of sweat go down my back.

I knew that Quantico was the home of the Weapons Training Battalion, which coordinates rifle and pistol qualifications for officers in the Marine Corps. I also knew it provided training and range support for the FBI, DEA, and IRS, as well as numerous state and local law enforcement agencies. It was also the home of the Marine Corps Sniper Instructor training. I had no doubt that Rodeo graduated top of his class in that course.

"When the helicopter arrives be ready, and I mean the both of you," Rodeo said.

With that, he stood, and we both watched as he strolled out of my office, but not before he and Velma exchanged one last, long look.

Velma then looked back at me and fumed out of my office.

"I told you," I heard her say, as I got up and watched Velma as she stood by our front window. I joined her, and we both watched Rodeo get into a large black SUV. I wasn't surprised when she gave him the finger as he got in the car. He just smiled and waved Velma a kiss good-bye.

"What was that all about?" I asked.

"What was what all about?" Velma said as she made her way back to her command station.

"You know what I mean, whatever it is that's between you two," I said.

"Don't ask," Velma said, as she picked up the phone and got back to work. "You don't want to know because then I'd have to shoot the both of you, and I'd hate to lose you."

Good thing she didn't have a gun. Velma, no doubt, could pull that trigger. Quantico, I thought.

Not sure they'd want Velma to set foot on that hallowed ground, though. I headed back to my desk and sat down, closing my eyes for a second. Velma had one more thing to say because, when I looked back up, there she was standing across from my desk and pointing her finger at me, just like my mother used to.

"Ernie was right, and the toes you stepped on were pretty big." She was really mad now and probably would later regret what she was telling me. I was quiet and held my breath.

"You've heard of J. Edgar Hoover and Richard Nixon–well those toes you stepped on wore the same shoe size."

With that, she went back up front, but not before she slammed shut the door to my office, leaving me alone with my thoughts.

I resumed breathing, closed my eyes for a moment, and shook my head. When I opened them, I looked at the door Velma had just slammed and my eyes caught something shiny on the floor. I got up, walked over and picked up a quarter.

I held onto the quarter for a moment, closed my eyes and I could almost hear my mother's voice: *You were too good at your job. You must have ruffled some feathers.*

"Thanks, Mom," I whispered. Well, at least I wasn't alone.

CHAPTER 10

I decided to head back to the mansion and dive headfirst into the books and records. The sooner I located Charlie the sooner I could exit from this mess. I had no desire to take up boot camp firearm training with Rodeo, or whatever else came along with the training, especially if Velma was nearby with a gun!

I told Velma to call Bruce and let him know I was heading over and that I'd probably be gone for the rest of the day. "Fine," she said. "Fine and dandy."

I knew there was no point in bringing Velma along since she was in a bad mood. Better to let her stew it out in the office. I didn't want her and Dominic to have another close encounter since there were already enough sparks flying around in her world.

I arrived at the mansion and walked in to find Bruce waiting to escort me to the office. He opened the closet door and motioned me in with a sweep of his arm. I followed him through the mansion, still in awe of the beauty of the house.

When we got to the office, Bruce said, "Here you go." And, then as he started to leave, he just couldn't contain himself from dispensing some fashion tips for me, "Look, girlfriend, your colors are all wrong. You should be wearing brighter colors and not hiding that bod of yours in that mousy dress for success suit. Don't you know that went out with disco?"

I stopped and looked at Bruce and held back my Greek temper and said, "Look, when I get a day off I'll ring you up, we'll have lunch and look at some color swatches. But, for now, these suits work just fine," I said with my thank you so much smile.

"Just fine for a librarian." With that he pivoted on his heels and sashayed out the door, but not without a final tip he probably got from his best bud, Aunt Anna.

"Okay, and we'll invite Jennifer to lunch. See if she could help you with your love life."

I watched him leave. Shaking my head, I walked straight over to the kitchen inside the mansion office and fixed myself a nice, comforting lunch.

As soon as I was done eating, I finished arranging the boxes, separating the ones we looked at the other day and the ones with the credit card information that still needed reviewing. My cell phone rang, and it was Velma.

"That's it, I may be turning in my resignation," Velma said.

Now what? I was thinking, "What, did Rodeo come back to tell us we were scheduled for the obstacle course training at Quantico?"

"No! Worse," she said. "Joe the Rusky just called. He and his pop, Boris, want to set up a luncheon date with you. They said to give their secretary a call and set it up."

Oh. This was going from bad to worse recalling the conversation I had with Ernie. "Boris wants to meet with me. I wonder what his angle is."

"I can only imagine," Velma said in a tone that meant she was rolling her eyes. "Have you ever heard the expression, 'If you lie down with dogs, you get up with fleas?' Well, MC, you are covered with fleas."

That immediately sent a vision to my brain, which didn't sit well with my stomach and the full lunch I had just eaten.

"Look, go ahead and set up the date with Boris and his son, Joe."

Velma took a deep breath on the other side of my cell and hung up, but not before I could hear her mumbling something about an exterminator.

I dialed Ernie on the cell number he had given Velma and me during our little chat. "What can you tell me about Boris and his son, Joe, that I don't know?"

"Why do you ask?" Ernie said.

"Because his people just called my people and want to set up a luncheon date."

Ernie was silent for a minute and then said, "Go ahead and set up the date, but let me know when and where, so I can alert Rodeo."

"Okay." For some reason, I was starting to itch.

"You already know what you need to know."

Silence.

"I'm still listening," I said.

"Boris came to Fish Camp about the time Dominic was whacked. He didn't order the hit if that's what you are wondering. Let's just say whoever ordered the hit told Boris to steer clear of Boca Vista after Dominic was hit," Ernie said. "That's really all you need and want to know for now. Contact me as soon as the meeting is set up," Ernie said.

"Wait a minute. I want to know if they are spooks like you," I said. It had been rumored that Boris and his family came to Fish Camp because he was KGB and was in their version of the witness protection program.

"You been spending too much time with Velma," he said with a laugh and then hung up. I had a funny feeling that the answer was yes.

*Great, now I feel hives breaking out on my legs.*

Velma called back and said she arranged the meet, and I could hear under her breath a mumble about looking for another job as soon as we found Charlie. Maybe something like working as Bruce's assistant.

I tossed my cell phone on the table and went back to reviewing the information in the boxes. I noticed after a while that something was missing, Charlie's appointment book or calendar.

The life of a CPA is driven by their appointments. To keep track of them, some had fancy, leather bound, appointment books, which they carted with them during the day. I carried a calendar, something nice and simple, I had carried over from my IRS days.

I spent the next hour or so going back through all the boxes with no luck. Finally, on my second try, I found it at the bottom of one of the boxes. I hadn't noticed it the first time because it didn't look like an appointment book. It looked more like a photo album. In fact, there was a picture of Charlie on the cover holding up a magnificent sailfish.

I looked at the picture and took it out of its sleeve. On the back, it said Costa Rica and the date, April 2009. It looked as if this was taken on one of Charlie's post tax season fishing trips, but instead of the Keys, this one was in Costa Rica. Well, both had good fishing. I put the picture back and started to flip through his appointment book.

For an accountant's appointment book, it was surprisingly empty, but with the rise of smartphones that do everything for you, I wasn't surprised.

He probably kept it more out of habit. It was the calendar for this year, so I skimmed from January through March and quickly over to April. I saw appointments for doctors and social events for him and Babbs. So, it looked as if he kept this book for personal appointments rather than business.

In April, I saw the appointment with Jennifer, and that was probably the date he dropped off that box of cash at her house. I flipped back to the beginning now that I had a feel for the appointment book, and close to the end of March, I saw where Charlie had penned in an appointment with the initials PI in caps. I kept going and found another one with PI and the date was April 16, the official end of tax season and about the time Charlie was heading out for his post tax season fishing vacation.

These appointments had to be with Harry West, the PI, who had been a friend of Ernie's. The same PI that went looking for Charlie when he didn't come home and the same PI whose death is now the center of an investigation, which included the feds. Charlie had written down the location of their appointments: Hotel Florida at the tiki bar. No surprise there.

I sat there and stared at the page for a minute and decided to call Ernie again and ask him about those appointments, particularly the one on April 16. I quickly looked through the rest of the appointment book, finding it mostly empty, while I waited for Ernie to answer. When he answered I could hear voices in the background, so he was tending bar.

"What's up?" was his greeting. I decided to get right to the point.

"When was the last time you saw Harry West?"

"About a week before his death," he said.

"Did he ever mention to you that he had an appointment with Charlie around the end of tax season?"

"He didn't mention it because he didn't have to. He was here that night, and Charlie stood him up," Ernie said. "Why?"

"Well, I'm looking through an appointment book of Charlie's, mostly personal stuff, and I see where he had two appointments with Harry West, one in late March and one on April 16, both at Hotel Florida."

"Hmm," Ernie said.

"I remember the first meeting because they met here but decided to go elsewhere and have a bite to eat," Ernie said.

"Did he ever say anything else to you about the reason for their meetings and why Charlie didn't show after that last meeting?"

Silence.

"Got to go," he said, and he hung up.

I sat there looking at my cell phone as if it was going to talk to me. Well, I wasn't going to get any more out of Ernie, so I made a mental note to ask Babbs what the family matter was and why that would have involved hiring a PI. I decided to wrap it up for the day and head home since it was getting late.

That evening, I went for another long run and thought about the day. Runs were a good time for thinking. Something was going on, and somehow it was all tied into this *Amazing Race* to find Charlie. I was hoping along the way I didn't run into a detour.

## CHAPTER 11

Velma didn't waste time. She set the meeting up for the morning of the next day. I was to meet with Boris and Joe in their office at the Full Moon. I knew Jennifer would already be there because she was interviewing entrants for next season's Fillies competition, which was going to be large since a lot of the girls had graduated and moved on to real jobs.

The waitresses were known as the Fillies. Most of them were college students paying their way through their masters and doctorates at Fish Camp University or FCU. They were hired for their sassiness and ability to be smartasses, but not offensive. It was a fine line, but Jennifer had them well trained.

Jennifer usually sang at the Full Moon and taught line dancing there during the week. It also didn't hurt business because it didn't take much to get Jennifer to also dance on the bar along with the team of Fillies.

That morning, I went straight from home to the Full Moon, and I was surprised to see Aunt Sophia and Aunt Anna and their crew from the public access studio on stage. I walked over to see what *Wayne's World* was up to.

"We're filming a shoot for the studio. We thought we would do a show on the Filly competition for the Full Moon. We are going to need some help with the interviews, are you interested?" Aunt Anna said.

"Ahh," I said. "I have a meeting with Boris and Joe about an accounting matter, maybe next time." With that, I made my getaway, but not before Aunt Anna corralled me between the main bar and the T-shirt store.

"Just a minute, I gotta talk to you, and you gotta listen."

When she was agitated, her English took on slang, kind of like the actors in the Humphrey Bogart movies she watched repeatedly. She knew all the lines, and thanks to Aunt Anna, so did I.

"What?" I said as I looked down at the munchkin I knew as my Aunt Anna.

"Aunt Sophia reread the cards last night, and you need to be very careful. We don't know exactly what you are involved in, but it's not safe," and then she added, "sister."

I took a deep breath here and rolled my eyes, but not before she added with a James Cagney inflection, "Aunt Sophia and I got your back."

"My back?" I asked as I leaned closer to my Aunt Anna's round face.

"Don't you remember the little chat we had the other night, Aunt Anna?" I whispered, knowing full well she did, but apparently, she planned to have selective memory or senior moments, as she called it.

"No, you and Aunt Sophia are not doing any such thing," I said. "You both need to keep your Greek noses out of this," I said firmly to the little munchkin in front of me.

"And tell Aunt Sophia to get a new deck of cards," I added, and since I was on a roll, "and Aunt Anna, you have to stop watching that cops and robbers channel." Aunt Anna loved cops and robbers shows and had been trying to get one of them from the cable channel to come to Fish Camp forever. So far, they had wisely resisted her offers. Thank you, St. Anthony, I thought.

My mother told me all about "Bribing Saint Anthony." She looked at me that day as if she was letting me in on a big secret, about the same way she looked at me when it came time to discuss the "birds and the beeswax" as she called it.

"Saint Anthony is a wonderful saint to have on your side."

"If you have a special request in your heart, then you pray to Saint Anthony for the hope that it might be granted. "Something big, you know like hoping your only child will land a good job or marry a good man." Ouch, I remember thinking at the time.

"And bring some dollar bills. Say a short prayer to Saint Anthony to grant your special request and then stick the dollar bills in the poor box. It's usually next to the holy water.

"It's better than lighting the candles," she continued with a wink as she reached into her luggage size purse and stuck some dollar bills in my hand and walked off.

I remember staring at her for a long time afterward, shaking my head.

"She had a dream," Aunt Anna said.

"Oh?" I said. Dreams are not good, so I usually pay attention to the dreams, since I have come to believe that those who have crossed the shore speak to us in our dreams.

"Your mother was in the dream, and she wasn't happy either."

"That's the dream. Mama was in the dream, and she wasn't happy?"

"Yes," Aunt Anna said. Well, nothing new there, I thought.

I spotted Joe out of the corner of my eye talking to Jennifer.

"Aunt Anna, I got to run. Please don't worry, its business, really," I said as I leaned closer to give her a hug and started to leave.

"In the cards … someone's dead."

I turned and went back to the munchkin who was giving me the nod of the head and the 'I told you so' eyeball look.

I leaned down and whispered to Aunt Anna, "Could she make out who it was?" I couldn't believe I was asking my aunt this question.

"No, but it was a man," Aunt Anna said.

"Oh good," I said to Aunt Anna. "Anybody we know?" Now I really could not believe I was asking my aunt this question!

Aunt Anna said something in Greek I couldn't make out, but I think the translation had the word stupid in it.

"Ok. I promise to be safe," I said since I saw real concern deep in her Greek eyes. With that, the munchkin smiled, reached up and gave me a hug. I watched her head back to her TV crew.

I walked over to where Joe and Jennifer were having what seemed to be a heated conversation, a lot of energy in the Full Moon for so early in the day.

They stopped their talking but eyed each other. I suspected it was another attempt at getting Jennifer to settle down with Joe and start making and raising little bambinos.

Jennifer always got that look in her eyes when she and Joe had the biological clock talk, and he pointed out her age. So far by my calculation, Jennifer would be good for a few more years so Joe would have to continue to pine.

Joe was a couple of years older than Jennifer and had been in love with her since the day he first saw her. He was heartbroken when she up and took off for Hollywood one day. He didn't count on her marrying the string of mafia lords, though.

Joe was the most eligible bachelor in town and had

the same good looks as Rodeo. But, he was still in love with Jennifer, who wasn't ready to settle down with Joe and become a wife and mother, at least not yet.

"MC, how are you doing?" Joe said.

"Couldn't be better," I lied. "How about you?" I said and smiled at Jennifer who was deep in thought.

Joe looked handsome, as always. Dark hair, dark eyes he looked more Greek than Russian. He was also tall and even taller with his cowboy getup.

"Won't you follow me?" he said, and to Jennifer "Let's talk later."

Jennifer spun on her heels and left in a huff and made a beeline to Aunt Sophia. Great, I thought, more card reading.

I just gave Joe a weak smile as he looked at Jennifer and back to me with a shake of the head. I then followed him to the Full Moon office where he held the door open for me to enter.

I had seen Boris several times over the years, but it had been awhile since I had seen him up close. As I entered the office, I was only a little surprised to see that he appeared shorter and much wider than I remembered.

In fact, he reminded me a lot of my own grandfather, Gus, sitting there behind a massive desk. He got up as I entered the room, came over with both of his hands extended, grabbed my hands and spread them apart to take a look at me like I was a member of the family he had not seen in a long while.

"MC, I am so happy to see you again. You look good. You have your mother's good looks but hopefully not your aunts' cantankerousness," he said, with a big smile and a wink of his amazingly blue eyes.

I was a little overwhelmed by the introduction and didn't know whether I should give him a big hug like I was seeing a relative from the family tree. The next thing I knew Boris was giving me a big hug, and I did my best to return it. But it was awkward, kind of like hugging a short, round oak tree.

"Come here. Come here," he said, and I followed him over to what looked like a conference table but laid out was a big spread. I thought I was back at my office at the mansion.

These people and their food, I thought, but I was a little hungry, and the food looked good.

"Eat. Eat. You don't have to worry about your weight, I see, not like me." With that, he patted his belly. Standing there, Boris looked like a miniature Buddha statue. The kind you see in Chinatown, and you're tempted to rub their belly to see if the genie appears. I wondered if Boris drove his car the same way as Babbs's Uncle Sal. We all found a seat at the conference table, and after we all had enough to eat and enough small talk, Boris got down to business.

"MC, I hear that you are looking for Charlie La-

Fleur."

I didn't have to respond because Boris kept on talking in between bites of a huge piece of apple pie he was wolfing down.

"I would also like to hire you to find Charlie." Then he added, "You see, Charlie has something of mine and I need it back."

This was definitely turning into *The Amazing Race*. For a moment, I thought about the cash that Jennifer was holding onto for Charlie and wondered if that was what Boris was talking about. I decided to take a defensive attack.

"What does Charlie have of yours?" I asked.

Boris looked at me and then at Joe and then back at me and in between finished off the apple pie.

He then took a big gulp of coffee, which I suspected had some vodka in it. Once again, he looked at Joe and then back at me.

Finally, with a big sigh, he said, "He has some very valuable cookbooks of mine. You see, Charlie was my CPA, and he also was a very talented chef. I loaned him my cookbooks to check out some recipes," he said, as he smiled at me. Then with some urgency, he added, "I need those cookbooks back."

I decided to keep silent and wait while I watched Boris take another swig of his coffee.

Boris looked at me and once again at Joe and then

back at me. Joe got up and opened the office door, looked out, and closed the office door. Boris took one more gulp of coffee and then spilled the beans.

"I will be honest with you, especially since you worked for the IRS. First and foremost, I want you to know how much I love this country. It has given me and my family rewards I could never have dreamed of in Russia. I pay my taxes and usually add a tip every year," he added with a big smile, and here he took a deep breath which oddly seemed to jiggle his enormous belly.

*Saint Anthony, please, I don't want to do CPR on this man.*

While I watched and listened, he took another deep breath and continued. The apple pie was calling my name, and whatever was in that coffee. "Charlie has possession of an essential set of books and records."

Here Boris paused and looked straight at me and said very clearly, "My cookbooks."

Boris stood and walked over to a bar in the corner of the room and poured himself a shot of vodka, slugged it down, and as if he knew, brought me back a big piece of apple pie.

"Thank you," I said, and took a quick bite before he continued.

"My cookbooks, I want you to know, were for purposes ... other than IRS filings," he said.

"Charlie maintained the books and records for IRS filings, but the cookbooks were for presentations to my upper management team, so to speak," he said. "I need those cookbooks back to present to my management team, and MC, I need them back ASAP, since our quarterly meeting is coming up in a few weeks."

Boris looked at me with a look on his face that told me unpleasant things would happen to him if he didn't get his *cooked books* back to present to his *upper management team.*

It didn't take an accounting degree to know he needed those *cooked books* back to show his *upper management team* a different bottom line.

"Well, I am already engaged to find Charlie, as you seem to know," and everyone else it seems like, I thought.

"So, I can't take on an engagement if it presents a conflict of interest to my *other client.*" Boris didn't flinch but took another sip from his coffee cup, which was empty.

"I understand that, but I am engaging you only to notify me if you find my cookbooks while going through the records for your search for Charlie. This should not present a conflict of interest with your other client," he said.

Then, as if reading my mind, he added, "Once the cookbooks are located, I will call on Ms. La-Fleur to arrange to pick up the books. Knowing the gracious woman Ms. La-Fleur is, it should be no problem, and then I will have my books available for my book club meeting," he said with a big belly laugh, which I thought was going to cause a tsunami.

*Yeah, you do not want those cooked books to fall into the hands of Dominic, you two have joined forces for now.*

"I just want you to look for those 'cookbooks' while you're going through the other books and records looking for Charlie, and then just let me know if they are in the records you are reviewing. I'll take it from there," he said, now serious and all business.

"No ethical conflict for you with your client, Ms. Babbs," Boris added. He got up, walked over to the food spread looking at it for a few seconds, and then came back waiting for my answer. Well, no secrets here, I thought. It seemed evident that they had been looking for these books, and to date, no one had found them, so they had concluded that they had to be in the boxes now sitting in the mansion office.

"In addition, you will have, at your disposal my son, Joe, and any other manpower you might need." And then he added, "In your search for Charlie."

So, there it was; in return for the tip as to the location of his cookbooks, he was offering to assist in the search for Charlie, something I am sure Babbs negotiated with him, also.

It was getting clearer by the minute that there was

far more to this search for Charlie, and it was getting more and more complicated by the moment. Good old Charlie was looking like the key to the search, instead of the object of the search.

Boris was speaking clearly between the lines and telling me that I had the pick of his manpower to hunt down and find Charlie, if that's what it was going to take to track down his cookbooks, before his quarterly business meeting with his upper management.

Here I was again, sitting in a room with people who were used to getting what they wanted one way or another, and they were waiting for my answer because they wanted something from me. They had each concluded that I was the best person to get the job done.

Boris looked over at Joe, who got up, walked over to the food spread and brought back a silver platter placing it in front of his father. Boris reached over and lifted the cover.

*Oh my, more cash!* I looked at a stack of money that was sitting on the platter. I guess I would have to make another trip to the deposit box on the way back to the office.

"I am going to pay you up front for the engagement," he said pointing to the cash, "to assist me in locating my cookbooks," he said, watching me intently.

"I am just asking you to go through the books you already have in your possession, and just let me know if you find my cookbooks. The money is yours to keep whether you locate them or not." Sitting there, I already knew my answer. I was already on the road, and it was too late to turn around and go back to the beginning and take another road. I just had to keep on going for now.

"All right," I heard myself saying. "I suppose I could look through the records, and if I locate your *cookbooks*, I will let you know."

"Good. Good," he said. "You are such a good girl, and you have your mother's lovely eyes and her beauty." With that, he came around and gave me the family hug and kiss on the cheeks and looked into my eyes and said, "And her wisdom." Well, I hadn't been called a girl in a long time and never had been called wise.

CHAPTER 12

I left through the back door of the Full Moon, to avoid my aunts and their public access crew. I carried with me my doggy bag of food and the doggy bag of cash and headed straight over to the bank to add to the hoard in my safe deposit box. I wasn't even going to count it. I had a funny feeling that I would find the cookbooks back at the mansion and that Boris knew for sure they were there.

Otherwise, he never would have admitted to me the existence of the second set of books. We left it that I would look for the books first and then contact Joe, and he would arrange the book club meeting with Babbs.

I stopped by the bank and got a second deposit box and placed the Boris cash in it. I decided I would keep the two hoards separate and when this was over, decide how much of this I would keep. It probably would depend on whether I needed a new identity or not.

When I got to the office,  waiting for me (or maybe really Velma), was Rodeo. He followed me into my office while Velma talked on the phone to her sister Cassie, who watched her twin girls during the day when not at school.

Rodeo shut the door and sat down in the chair across from me and called Ernie on his really smart cell to set up a telephone conference. The next thing I knew, a life-size image of Ernie appeared on the wall of my office.

Out of the corner of my eye, I could see the yacht, *Pirate Life*, docked out back. I closed my eyes, took a deep breath and tried to transport myself on board, but when I opened my eyes, Ernie was still on the wall and Rodeo was still sitting across from my desk.

I knew spooks had spy stuff and all, but this was way over my dorky head. I heard Ernie's voice as clear as if he was in my office sitting next to Rodeo.

"You will find the *cookbooks* in the records back at the mansion, and it's okay to let Boris know at that point."

Somehow, I wasn't surprised that Ernie and Rodeo were already up to speed on the meeting I'd just had with Boris.

"So, the office at the Full Moon is bugged?"

Silence was again my answer.

"We are positive now that the information we need to find Charlie is in the books and records you have from Babbs. You just do your thing and find him by going through those records. They will lead to Charlie. Boris's cookbooks just happened to be mixed into with the soup."

"Look you two, I want to know what's really going on, and I'm not going any further until someone tells me the real case and how Charlie got mixed up in all this jazz," I said.

Saying that made me immediately feel better. And, I was going to wait until either Ernie or Rodeo gave me an answer.

I watched as there was a pause and then an okay nod from 3D Ernie to Rodeo. "We will talk later," 3D Ernie said directly to me, and then disappeared.

Rodeo closed his cell then turned to me and said without missing a beat, "We have good intelligence that there is a terrorist plot to take down a significant historic structure."

"You do?" I said. "So that's why you guys are involved? You got me running around in circles looking for Russian cookbooks and a guy who probably lost track of time and is still fishing and drinking somewhere in the islands." After a pause to blink his eyes, followed by a deep breath, he continued.

"We're not talking about buildings like the twin towers, but a major patriotic symbol, something that, if destroyed, would shake the country to its roots. I'll refer to this operation as Stars and Stripes. We don't know where or what it is exactly, but we have a pretty firm idea about who is involved," Rodeo continued as I listened intently.

"You do?" I said again. After another blink Rodeo continued.

"There is a freelance group of covert operatives known as the Green Team," he said. "Chatter out there tells us they are mixed up in this plot to take down a structure that is a major patriotic symbol. We are sure, though, that it will take place in the next few months since we are nearing another anniversary of 9/11."

I just sat there and stared at Rodeo, who looked as if he was contemplating whether or not to tell me something more and he had already told me a lot.

Rodeo was sitting there staring out at *Pirate Life*. I was quiet and took a quick peek at the window to see if Izzy was there, but he wasn't. When I looked back, Rodeo had closed his eyes for a moment, and then he opened them, looked at me and then took the plunge.

I heard him say "dang it" under his breath as he pulled his chair closer to my desk. Having decided in his mind that he was going to tell me more, he continued, but it came with stipulations.

"What I am about to tell you, MC, I will deny I ever said. You need to understand this because it is highly classified information, and I am only telling you because I don't want anything to happen to you or—" and here he took another deep breath, "—Velma. Do you understand?" he said.

I nodded my head and whispered, "Yes, I do."

"Good," Rodeo said.

"Does this include Ernie?" I said.

He looked deep into my eyes and said, "That includes anyone."

I now sat there quiet as a church mouse, but it didn't

take a rocket scientist to know that the reason he was telling me this was only because Velma was involved.

Rodeo continued, "We don't know who has bought their services, but we think Charlie La-Fleur may have crossed paths with whoever hired the Green Team. That is why we need to find him, find out what he knows, and stop this plan. The Green Team, by the way, is a team of four operatives, sometimes referred to in the circles they run in as The Unmentionables," Rodeo said.

He paused for a minute to let that sink in, which it did like an anchor around my waist in deep dark water.

"They are the best at what they do, and they work for the highest bidder regardless of affiliation, which is also why, in those same circles, they are referred to as the four sluts. After 9/11, the U.S. government, in all its wisdom, decided to give them secure government jobs," Rodeo said.

"Just like the one you had at the IRS," he said, as he pointed his finger at me.

There it was again, my mother seemed to have this ability to channel these messages to me. I just sighed and continued to listen.

"They were given clearance to do whatever was needed to carry out the mission of tracking down terrorists and thwarting any plots that would lead to another 9/11. They were highly trained by the best, the U.S. military, and they are very, very, dangerous.

"Homeland Security had been the parking spot for these types of covert agents, so they could carry out their assignments under the radar, so to speak," Rodeo said.

*Homeland Security, hmmm, that parking lot seems to be filling up lately.*

"Only a small handful of individuals within the government are privy to this information," Rodeo said. He paused again. I could see his mind working, that same look, considering how much he was going to tell me, looking out the window at the water. He was looking at something only he could see, but whatever it was he decided to go on and tell me the rest of the story.

"They take their orders from some individual high up in the Department of Justice. It's the same person who oversaw the IRS and their part in the war on terrorism."

Rodeo gave me time to digest this and then ask. "Is that the same person whose toes I stepped on?"

"Yes," Rodeo said. "You stepped on them all right, and that is why we are having this conversation, and why I am sharing this information with you and Velma. It's not the bad guys you need to watch out for, it's the good guys."

"So that last case I worked on regarding that innocent spouse claim may have triggered losing my job?" I asked.

Rodeo just looked at me without saying a word. If that was true, then the whole story that the IRS was being used to audit and harass individuals for political purposes, now began to make sense.

Rodeo continued, "Let's just say that your work put that individual in a very precarious position. You know who he is, Walther Roosevelt, the U.S. Attorney for the DOJ who heads the war on terror program. Right after 9/11, he was handpicked to oversee the operations for the DOJ to fight the war on terror. It was his job to coordinate this war with other federal agencies. The right hand still didn't know what the left hand knew, but he did, and so he was in a very influential position."

"He was?"

"He was, but time has passed, and both you and I know the war on terror has taken a back seat to the economy and other, more pressing issues," Rodeo said.

I still felt like Rodeo was leaving something out, which is the way I usually felt when carrying on a conversation with either he or Ernie.

"But how did you find this out?"

Rodeo blinked his eyes and then said, "Velma."

"Velma?" I said somewhat loudly.

"Only Ernie and I know this, but Velma and your boss, of the IRS Marathon office, also figured it out."

He then leaned a little closer to my desk, as if he didn't want Velma to hear what he was about to say.

"Let's just say Velma blurted it out one day while we were having a heated conversation about something else you really don't need to know about," Rodeo said with a big sigh and the head nod.

"So there, MC is the bit of knowledge Ernie promised you so you can stop wondering for the rest of your days why you lost your job. You were just at the wrong place at the right time, did your job a little too well for some folks, and ruffled some big feathers," he said.

*Wow, I hear an echo.*

"Always remember, knowledge is like those free-weights you work out with. It can build muscle and make your muscles strong. Or, if you aren't careful, they can also tear that muscle and put you on the bench for a while.

"But, let's get back to operation Stars and Stripes," he said smoothly and before I had a chance to think much about what he'd just said. "Okay, Okay," I said. He was running way too fast for me.

"Let me think about what you are telling me for a second. First of all, there is a plot to take down something that is dear to the hearts of all Americans, symbolic like the Stars and Stripes or Old Glory. But since we've already seen Old Glory burned more than once on TV, it's something else."

"Yes," Rodeo said.

"Okay," I said and continued.

"But we don't know what or where, but we suspect that these Green Team operatives, also known as the four sluts, may be involved," I said.

"Correct," he said.

"OK," I said.

"Then you are telling me that I lost my job and the IRS shut down my office and the whole tracking of terrorist operations because of the innocent spouse claim I worked on before I was let go?"

"Yep," he said, and once again leaned a little closer to my desk. "But, you can take that up with Velma. For now, let's just stick with the Stars and Stripes operation."

"Do you and Ernie have proof of that whole situation and Walther Roosevelt's involvement?" I asked out of maybe that psychic side of my brain my aunts are after me to open.

Rodeo just gave me a long hard look which I interpreted as yes or maybe. He wasn't going to tell me until the time was right.

Trying to focus, I was sitting there thinking out loud trying to put this all together. Something was missing, so I asked Rodeo.

"How do you know all this Stars and Stripes stuff?" I asked.

"I mean, I know you and Ernie are still connected with Homeland Security or whomever you guys work for, but why am I involved in all this? What's the connection?"

Rodeo just looked at me, but I could see on his face he had already crossed the line in the sand, and he actually looked relieved, as if it felt good talking to someone about what he was about to tell me.

"Harry West, the PI," he said.

"Oh brother, Harry West," I said. I sat there for a second and now I was looking out at *Pirate Life*.

"Harry West," I said and went on, "who I am correct now in assuming was more than just a PI, uncovered the plot to take down Stars and Stripes and somehow along the way that got him killed."

"That's right," Rodeo said.

"But how?" I said.

"We are not sure, but that's why we need to find Charlie. We are pretty sure Charlie was the last person to see Harry West before he was murdered."

We both sat there now looking at *Pirate Life*.

When I worked on these investigations in the Marathon office, I had worked from the safety of the four walls of my IRS office, which was guarded by the far-reaching powers of the IRS.

Those powers extended even to those at the top

levels of government. I was always given complete access to any books and records I needed, but I also had no contact with the agents who worked in the field, the Green Team guys. Their part was just known as "fieldwork."

I never met the agents in the field or actually even knew the true nature of their assignments.

If I ever had any questions, we had a contact on the Criminal Investigation side of the IRS. Thinking back now, it was Velma who would take the questions and get back to us with answers. That suited me just fine. I now was beginning to realize just how much sensitive information Velma was privy to and how much she must know about these covert operations.

"But how does Charlie fit into all this?" I asked, still staring at *Pirate Life*.

"When you find Charlie, we hope to get an answer to some of those types of questions," Rodeo said, as he now got up and walked over to the window to get a closer look at *Pirate Life*.

"Oh," I said as I watched him.

"That's all you need to know for now," Rodeo said still staring at *Pirate Life*.

Turning to face me Rodeo continued, "MC, don't worry." He walked back to stand in front of my desk. "I am telling you this only as a precautionary measure. It's just like the firearms training, we will be doing shortly.

Just between you and me, you have the power of the U.S. military behind you. You are being watched over. You may feel like you are alone, but you're not."

And then he got serious. "You know, I would never let anything happen to you or Velma. Let's just say I have a personal stake in the matter." Just then, I flashed on the realization that Velma's girls looked a lot like Rodeo.

"We've got your back." With that, he made his exit stage right.

I sat there for a long while taking in this conversation. Well now, I thought. I have Rodeo, Ernie, the U.S. military, even Joe and Boris, Aunt Anna and Aunt Sophia looking out for me. My money is on Aunt Sophia and Aunt Anna.

## CHAPTER 13

I came out of my stupor and went up front to talk to Velma. A little voice told me now was not the time to get into a conversation with Velma about Rodeo and what he had told me about Walther Roosevelt. That would have to wait. Now was the time to tackle the rows of boxes that sat on the conference table and spilled over to the floor in the office, back at the mansion. Somewhere, in those boxes, was Charlie.

Although it was getting late, I told Velma I was heading back to the mansion for a few hours, and I wasn't coming back until I found a lead on Charlie's sorry ass. She waved good-bye as I left her deep in thought, as she usually was after spending time with Rodeo.

The first thing I needed to do was find those cookbooks and get that little complication out of the way. I didn't need my inner voice to tell me that Dominic was also interested in finding them. It was becoming apparent to all that he had his own ambitious plans for the grocery business and was just cooling his heels, waiting to take over when the time was right.

Those cookbooks would give him leverage over Boris and his operations in Fish Camp, and without Charlie in the way, he was set to muscle Babbs out of the way and take over as soon as his father, Sal, kicked the bucket.

A thought had also started to enter my mind about Dominic and how convenient it was that Charlie had not returned from his fishing trip. It was parked in the back of my mind, on the back burner, so to speak. Right now, it was time to pour over the credit card statements to see if they held any clues to Charlie's whereabouts.

When I worked my cases with the IRS, I started just as I did with Babbs, by going through the taxpayer's books and records.

It was like reading someone's diary. Unless they dealt 100 percent in cash, which is very difficult, they always left a paper trail. In IRS circles, what was used to follow this paper trail was something known as a T account.

You didn't need an accounting degree to put together a T account, plain old common sense worked just fine. There was a reason for this. If the T account needed to be explained by a government attorney in a court of law, the jury could easily follow along and conclude that the defendant was cheating on his taxes.

You simply started by drawing a large *T* on a legal-size piece of paper. On the right side of the *T*, you list expenses, and on the left side, you list income. Theoretically, the two column totals should match.

As an agent, I would go through the taxpayer's checks and bank statements and list all their expenses for categories like rent, mortgage, food, child care, and cash on one side, and then I went back through and listed known sources of income on the other side.

The income would be wages or business income, sales of houses, properties or cars and other sources such as loans, transfers from other bank accounts and last year's tax refund. You list these items on their respective side of the T account, total the two sides of the T account and compare the bottom line.

Logically, the T account should balance. The total for the taxpayer's income (taxable or nontaxable) should be more or close to equal to the money spent to cover expenses for the year. If not, the taxpayer had a little explaining to do. Where did he get the cash to cover the expenses for the year, and why doesn't that amount show up on his tax return for the year?

If he couldn't explain the difference with a source of nontaxable income, like a loan, then the IRS would assume (especially if he was in a cash business) that the difference was taxable income and eventually he would receive a bill for the additional taxes along with hefty penalties and interest.

If it was a considerable amount, and if he had gone to great lengths (other than sloppy bookkeeping) to hide the extra income (concealed bank accounts), he was threatened with the possibility of going to jail. At a minimum, he would have hefty attorney's fees to pay to get him out of his mess with the IRS.

It wasn't unusual for the taxpayer (and/or their legal representatives) to come up with, what is called in IRS circles, a cash hoard alibi. This served as an explanation for the difference, which the IRS called an understatement of income. Here, again, you really didn't need an expensive legal team to come up with this alibi as an explanation for the out of balance T account because sometimes it was true and not a cooked-up alibi.

I could buy a cash hoard story because I knew both my aunts and my mother before them; kept cash in their safe deposit boxes, and the only thing that went in the bank account was their social security checks.

Right now, I was thinking about Charlie's cash hoard as I made my way back to the mansion. Was it sitting in that box in Jennifer's secret room? Velma had called ahead, and Bruce met me and once again escorted me to my office away from home. This time he didn't want to chat or throw barbs. He just left me to get to work, which was a relief.

I started right away by creating the T account to track down Charlie, though I was not looking for unreported income as an IRS agent would.

In Charlie's case, I was looking for clues as to his whereabouts and whatever else fell out along the way, like an explanation to his cash hoard.

I was hoping it would reveal a pattern or a trail that would give me a lead on Charlie's fishing hole. If I did come up with a T account that did not balance, it would just imply that Charlie had another source of income. It could be anything from a nest egg he was accumulating for his retirement or cash entrusted to him for safekeeping. It might have something to do with Charlie's disappearance or nothing to do with it. It could be something else Charlie was entrusted with, like Boris's cookbooks.

It could be anyone starting with Babbs and Uncle Sal, not to mention Ernie and his employer, the U.S. government. I would have to warn Jennifer again to keep mum about the box in her secret closet.

Either way, it was becoming clear to me that everyone was looking for Charlie, but maybe for different reasons. Babbs was looking for Charlie because he was long overdue coming home. Or maybe she and her Uncle Sal had another reason for finding Charlie. The family might be looking for cash gone missing.

Maybe they also had a quarterly management meeting coming up and needed the cash for their quarterly meeting, cash that Charlie was laundering for Babbs and her family. Maybe Jennifer had that cash sitting in her secret closet. Maybe they had a balloon note due soon, and they needed that cash to make the payment.

Boris needed his cookbooks back for his board of directors meeting coming up soon, or he would have major problems. The U.S. government was looking for Charlie because the feds thought he somehow got himself mixed up with a plot to take down Stars and

Stripes.

For me, I was hoping the books and records would lead me to Charlie so I could get back to my *normal* life. I sat down and dove into the books head first to see where they would take me.

CHAPTER 14

I spent most of the rest of the day and into the late evening holed up in my office at the mansion pouring over the books and records and making countless trips to the spread laid out on the buffet table. By the end of the evening, I was stuffed but had finished the T account.

To my surprise and dismay, it didn't produce an understatement of income. In fact, the T account balanced. This told me that the briefcase, that Jennifer recognized as a brand that usually held cash, delivered to her for safekeeping did not come from either Charlie or Babbs's personal or business accounts. At least not from the bank accounts and records that Babbs supplied me with to review. At that point, I decided to visit the mansion's liquor cabinet in my office.

As I sipped a glass of wine and looked out at the waves crashing on the beach, I thought my results through. There could be, no doubt, other books and records that Babbs had not supplied to me. They were, in all likelihood, Babbs's own set of cookbooks. The other odd finding of the evening was that I did not find Boris's cookbooks. Their presence had been pretty much a given, according to Ernie. I concluded from that that someone had entered the office, located and removed them before I could find them, but who? Who would have known about them and also had access to this room?

The person that came to mind was Dominic. He had the motive, for sure, and could use them to his advantage. He was young and ambitious and not tied to the agreements of older family members.

I had not found anything out of the ordinary in the personal expenses and credit card statements that would reflect another side of Charlie, the scoundrel side. It was a known fact that Charlie was a wheeler-dealer, so a money trail leading to some cockamamie investment wouldn't have surprised me.

If Charlie were a gambler or had other women on the side, a paper trail wouldn't have been far behind. But, I found nothing, nada. He was as squeaky clean as an altar boy.

I could only go by the records that were given to me. More times than not, the records that are handed over will have a clue that leads you to those undisclosed records. Sooner or later their paths cross.

The back of a check will show a deposit of that check to a different bank account or a wire transfer from an offshore account to a stock account or vice versa. It's inevitable.

Somehow the money that goes into one account makes its way to another account, one way or another. The number one red flag is cash deposits. I scoured the records I was given for those clues and came up empty.

That left me with the cash hoard theory, the money that never made its way into the bank accounts, hidden or not. A cash hoard, cash sitting in a safe, under a mattress, a coffee can buried in the backyard, in the family pet cemetery, or sitting nice and snug in a safe deposit box inside the walls of a bank.

The only conclusion I had reached by the end of the day was that Charlie had a cash hoard, either his or someone else's and for some reason, he had decided Jennifer was the best person to sit on it.

Since he was also Jennifer's CPA and financial mentor, it's not unlikely that Jennifer had told him about the secret room in her mansion. As for the cookbooks, I decided to put them out of my mind for the moment and make that call in the morning. The little voice inside my head was already giving me a migraine.

I was getting tired and getting hungry again despite the carb overload I had devoured at the buffet in my mansion office. My brain was shutting off, mellowed by the wine, so I decided to head out of the mansion and head home.

I was sure that Aunt Sophia and Aunt Anna had something good to eat on the burner, so I decided to drop in and check on them and, of course, they would be glad to feed me.

On the way out, for some reason, my mind led me back to Charlie's appointment book and the picture on the front of the book. I picked it up to take another took and just stared at it for the longest time, hoping it would talk to me.

So that year he was in Costa Rica for his end of tax season getaway, but this year he told Babbs he was heading to the Keys. Maybe he didn't head to the Keys after all but headed back down to Costa Rica instead. I went back to the most recent credit card statements and took another look at the charges.

I had seen where he had purchased some fishing equipment shortly after he left for his trip, but assumed it had been purchased in the Keys. Babbs had told me he went to the Keys, and I had not found any airline tickets to another destination, so I had assumed he went to the Keys. Sometimes, making an assumption is almost like putting blinders over your eyes.

I found the charge and studied it closer. The name of the place was Hector's Bait and Tackle. I went over to the computer and tried to Google Hector's Bait and Tackle and Keys and found no hits. So, I decided to try Costa Rica, and there it was a link for Hector's Bait and Tackle in Costa Rica. Charlie had not gone fishing in the Keys; he had gone to Costa Rica. I was just getting ready to call Ernie and tell him about the lead on Charlie when I felt someone's presence behind me, and before I could turn around, I heard Dominic's voice.

"How is it going? Burning the midnight oil, are you?"

As I turned to look at him, I could see that he had his eyes on the computer screen.

"Fine," I said and hit the keys to lock the screen.

Dominic and I just locked eyes for a long moment, and then he smiled.

"Well, MC, I saw the light in the office and was just dropping by to see if there was anything you needed," he said as he smiled, but his eyes took in the desk where the computer sat and the appointment book with the picture of Charlie on the cover.

He walked over and picked up the appointment book and looked at the picture of Charlie and then turned to me and said very seriously, "You know, MC, my Aunt Babbs is a very busy woman and works very hard for the town of Boca Vista. She enjoys her role as Queen, and the town returns the affection. Marrying Charlie was a mistake, and I am telling you this out of love for my aunt."

"Their marriage was more of an arrangement. As my father's health was failing, Charlie showed up and charmed her. As we all know, he is a charmer, and before long, he stepped in and was running the family business."

"But, I am here now, and it is only right that a family member run the business and not an outsider whose motives for marrying my aunt are suspect, in my opinion," he said, and then he stepped in and delivered his message point blank while handing me the appointment book.

"MC, you might find that Charlie has not disappeared, but has, let's say, moved on, and that may not be such a bad thing for my aunt and our family."

I just stared at him for what seemed to be the longest moment and did my best not to blink. I then stood and faced him and heard myself say, "I will take that into consideration, Dominic," I said, and then added, "and your affection for your aunt, of course."

I'm not sure where the gumption came from to stand up to Dominic right then, but I was not going to let him bully me from doing my job. Of course, knowing I had Ernie and Rodeo watching my back probably helped.

"Just so we have an understanding," he said, as he stepped a little closer to my face. "I wouldn't want to see her, or anyone else, get hurt," he said.

With that, he smiled and walked over to the half empty buffet table and added, as he walked out the door without even looking at me, "I see you need more food. I will tell the staff."

I looked at the door for the longest time and decided to take the appointment book with the picture of Charlie with me, so I stuffed it into my briefcase.

Well, Dominic had delivered his message to me, and it was clear that he was telling me that if I didn't find Charlie, it would be a good thing for all, and I guess that meant me, also.

I was glad he had laid his cards on the table, and I knew where he stood, just where we had suspected.

He was here to take over the grocery business from Babbs as soon as the time was right for him. He was right, though, about Charlie. He was a wheeler-dealer, and for all I knew, the cash he had left with Jennifer may have been his buyout from Dominic.

He may very well be sipping rum while fishing in Costa Rica. That's fine, I thought, but I wanted to see it with my own eyes, and it looked as if a trip to Costa Rica was in order for Ernie or Rodeo. I would give them a call in the morning and bring them up to speed on Charlie and my conversation with Dominic.

For now, I was heading out the door of the mansion and maybe an early morning jog to burn some of those calories off considering all the food I had eaten at the buffet table, which Dominic just had to mention in his own Bruce fashion that he would be re-stocking.

CHAPTER 15

On my way back to my condo, even though it was close to midnight, I saw the light was still burning at my aunts' and decided to stop by and check in on those two. When I got to their door, I could hear laughter and talking going on and decided to leave, but before I could, Aunt Anna opened the door.

She and Aunt Sophia probably were peeking out the windows and saw my car pull up. Over her shoulders, I saw most of their public access crew, and they were eating and talking and just plain having a good old time.

Aunt Anna said, "We're hosting a potluck for the crew to go over last-minute plans for the convention next week. Come on in, we have plenty of food, and everyone will be glad to see you."

I had almost forgotten about their annual trip to the public access convention held every year in New York City at the Waldorf. Great, more food, I thought, I'll be getting up early for a longer jog.

As I walked in, I could see the group that had made up my mother's public access crew sitting around the sofa laughing while they told their stories from the library of life. My aunts had taken over the role of their leader from my mother. The average age was 85, but their mental age was not anywhere near that, and they were pretty spry for their actual age. They all rushed up and gave me hugs, and, right then, those hugs felt good. They were of the age that they didn't have to rush off and catch up with the rest of their life. They had lived long enough to know that life is lived in the here and now, and they knew that, for them, the minutes of their lives were limited.

In that respect, they shared my mother's outlook on life. The glass of life was always half full for them and never half empty. This group was always laughing, dancing, singing, and joking. I had let down my guard and had become their friend when my aunts took over the leadership role.

At times like this, when they were all there talking about their public access shows, it seemed almost as if I could catch a glimpse of my mother out of the corner of my eyes, sitting there with them, laughing and joking. My mother had been known for having a loud and infectious laugh, a real belly laugh. It had been contagious.

I would look quickly while laughing with them to see if I could catch her spirit, but she was too quick. I kept looking just the same.

We ate abundant amounts of food and drank Greek wine and told jokes, and by the end of the evening, it was Aunt Anna, Aunt Sophia and what I would call their core group, the group that was up to anything and just waiting for the word from my aunts.

Sitting on the very end of the couch were Molly and

Harold. Molly, whose career as a Broadway dancer kept her, at 82, still looking and moving like a dancer. Her red hair cut short with bangs that framed her blue eyes that looked out between her freckles. Molly was a spitfire, and as a result, she and Aunt Anna seemed to butt heads. I sometimes wondered if it was because Aunt Anna was secretly smitten with Harold.

Sitting next to Molly was her shadow, Harold. Besides being smitten with Molly, he was a true gentleman in every sense of the word. Harold was 85, retired military and had served in the big one as a general. Molly, at her age, wasn't interested in any romantic involvements (or so she said), but still, she and Harold were good friends and spent a lot of time together, mainly because Harold followed her everywhere, including to the public access studio.

Rounding out the core group was Velma's Aunt Sadie. Aunt Sadie was Velma's mother's twin sister. They were as different as night and day. Velma's mother was as sweet as sugar and was very much a homebody, and her social life centered on her church and her family. Aunt Sadie was the opposite: a spiritual woman, but not a church lady. She was tough and independent and not a homebody. This explained why she had been married several times in her life.

Aunt Sadie was a force to reckon with, and even Aunt Sophia and Aunt Anna would bow to her at times to avoid a skirmish. By the nature of their personalities, there was a continual power struggle between Aunt

Sophia and Velma's Aunt Sadie when it came to their public access show.

Next to Aunt Sophia, Aunt Sadie had been my mom's best friend, and she took a particular interest in me after my mom died. After Aunt Sophia and Aunt Anna, I was the closest to Aunt Sadie.

As I was in the kitchen returning my glass and plate to get ready to head home, I heard Aunt Sophia say, "Your mother came to me last night in a dream." Oh boy, not the dream. This must be the dream Aunt Anna brought up when I saw her earlier at the Full Moon.

"She didn't have time to talk because she had a big show going on." Oh yes … it continues at the next level apparently.

"She did send you a warning to be very careful, and I think she still wants you to settle down and find a good man and stay married this time."

I wonder how much of the message was edited by my aunts to include the settling down part. If I was able to pin them down, I half expected them to say, "Oh yeah, I added that part."

Aunt Sophia continued, "She has directed us to continue to watch over you, and so whatever you are up to, you might as well know I will be watching your back."

Terrific, I thought. It was time to at least attempt to wrap this little potluck dinner up, or at least try so I could get some rest.

I had a feeling that tomorrow was going to be a busy day, and I really did not have the energy to get into a discussion with my Aunt Sophia about her dreams.

"Okay, okay," I said.

"Listen," I heard my voice, which held a degree of calmness I knew was not there, "I appreciate your concern and I respect your dreams, but you really have nothing to worry about," I continued as I gave her a hug. She handed me a doggie bag on my way out.

Aunt Sophia, to my relief, then said, "We'll talk later. You look tired and need your rest. Go on home and get some rest."

She was right; I was too tired to carry on this conversation any longer. I said good night and hugged everyone. Aunt Anna saw me to the door and stuffed another take-home meal in my hands.

"We love you." That's all she said. I gave her a hug and went home. I was bushed but had a crazy dream about my aunts and their public access crew and Rodeo and Ernie and some bad guys. In the dream, Aunt Sadie was in charge with Harold hunting down the bad guys. It was a real nightmare which I hoped was not an omen.

CHAPTER 16

The next morning, I woke early and couldn't get back to sleep, so I got up and went for a long jog to burn off those calories from yesterday's meals.

Afterward, I decided to head straight back to the mansion to see if I could wrap up the books and records and find those cookbooks before Dominic. I got to the mansion and located some of the housekeeping crew who let me in the door that led to my office in the mansion, and I made my way through the house.

When I got to the office, I opened the door, and there was Bruce with a duster in his hand standing over the boxes on the conference table. Without turning, he said, "Well, you're here bright and early."

"How did you know it was me?" I said.

"Security cameras, my dear," as he walked over and set up the coffee pot.

"I guess I could say the same for you. What are you doing here so early?" I said, with the emphasis on the word *here*.

With that, Bruce walked over to me and handed me the duster and said, "My day never ends." I watched as he sashayed out the door.

What a bitch, I thought, and made my way over to the boxes Bruce was dusting. As I looked closer, I saw what looked like some more records added to the mountain of records already housed in this office. Great, I thought; more records to review.

As I stepped closer to the very top of the pile, my jaw dropped because my little voice was telling me, before I even looked, that sitting on top of the pile were Boris's cookbooks. I looked closer and confirmed my theory.

Well, I thought. That was interesting. The cookbooks had been returned to the office sometime between the time I left last night and my arrival this morning to find dear old Bruce dusting away.

I started to turn around and almost bumped right into Bruce. We just stared at each other for a moment, and then I pointed the duster to the books and said, "I see you uncovered some more books and records."

"Yes," he said. "Joe is on his way over to pick them up and return them to the library."

"Oh, that's good," I said. Where did you find them?" I asked.

"Let's just say ... in unfriendly territory," he added.

With that, he picked up the books and said, "I will see that they are delivered to the library, and no fines are paid."

"Thanks," I said.

"No problem," he said and picked some imaginary lint off the front of my suit jacket.

Since now seemed as good a time as any to discuss Dominic with him, "Bruce."

"Yes," he said, as he now was walking behind me and picking more lint off my suit jacket.

"What do you think of Dominic?"

Bruce was now standing in front of me as he leaned close and whispered, "He's evil. Stay out of his way, for your own good." A very pregnant pause went by before he said, "Got to go."

With that, he walked right out the room, cookbooks in hand. My cell rang and when I answered it was Boris. News travels fast.

"Thank you, my dear," he said. "I will be forever in your debt," and was about to hang up when I asked, "Do you have friends in Costa Rica?" "Why yes, my dear, I have family in Costa Rica."

"Really," I said, and before I could formulate my thoughts Boris added,

"I'd be happy to inquire about the fishing in Costa Rica."

"That would be great."

"No problem," he said. "Have a great day," and then he hung up.

The coffee pot finished it's gurgling, so I walked over and poured myself a cup. As I drank my coffee, I thought, well, that was easy enough. Bruce will see that the cookbooks are returned to their proper owner. I'll wait and see what Boris and his family can tell me about Charlie and the fishing in Costa Rica. Hopefully, this family soap opera will come to an end soon with Charlie's return, and I can bow out and go back to my tax practice and leave the covert stuff to Ernie and Rodeo.

I had just finished my cup of coffee and was about to get back to the books and records when my cell beeped. This time it was Velma.

"Bruce called and set up a meeting this afternoon at one, back here at the office, for Babbs to meet with you to go over something and he implied the environment would be more conducive to discussion at your office than the mansion."

"Really," I said.

"Yes, really," she said. "See you later," and she hung up the phone.

I spent the rest of the morning wrapping up my work on the books and headed back to the office where I was greeted by Velma up front on the phone, "They're waiting for you," she mouthed with her hand over the mouthpiece and nodding her head in the direction of my office.

"They," I said.

"Yes," she whispered. "The Queen brought Bruce," and she returned to her phone conversation.

Well, no surprise there, I thought, as I headed into my office where they sat waiting for me. I felt as if I was late for the meeting, but actually, I was early. I walked around and sat down at my desk, and before I could give them a proper howdy-do, Bruce got up, walked over and shut the door to my office and returned to his seat.

I waited for the Queen to start the meeting.

"Thank you, my dear, for locating the books for Mr. Rusky. I'm learning a little more about Charlie's business in his absence, and the matter of returning his records was of the utmost importance to him, so I'm glad I was able to assist," Queen Babbs said.

"Yes," I said looking at Bruce. "I'm glad I was able to help. I may need to get my eyes checked because I must have been looking right at them, but with all the records they blended in, I suppose." The small talk seemed to come easy in my office today.

Silence, and then Bruce spoke.

"Actually, your eyesight is fine because they were not included in the books and records we supplied you with, they were in Dominic's possession," he said. "He must have returned them late last night because they were there first thing in the morning when I stopped by your office to set up coffee and bring in more food."

"Oh," I said. "Thank you. I mean, for the food."

"You're welcome. But I would watch the Danish,"

he added.

I just glared at him, wondering just like I did the other day where this meeting was headed. It seemed like I was just along for the bus ride, waiting patiently for my stop.

The Queen took over.

"MC, I am here to talk to you about Dominic. For what I'm about to tell you, it's best we talk here at your office instead of the mansion," she said.

Great, I thought, now we're making headway.

"My uncle's health has been failing for the past year, and more and more the duties of running the grocery business have fallen on me. When Charlie and I married he maintained his tax practice, but as Uncle Sal's health failed, Charlie took on more and more of the duties running the day-to-day operations of the grocery business. This was a great comfort to me," she said.

"I assumed this would be temporary. I had hoped for the best, which was that Uncle Sal regaining his health and returning to run the business 100 percent," she said. while looking at Bruce from time to time, who nodded with encouragement and listened patiently out of respect for a story he certainly had heard before.

At this point, she stopped, and like Rodeo the other day was staring out the window at *Pirate Life*. This seemed to be Bruce's key to take over the storytelling.

"Since Dominic has returned, Ms. Le-Fleur has been experiencing flashbacks of her father's death," Bruce said.

Oh my, I thought.

"I assume having grown up in Fish Camp you had heard the story of her father Dominic and his murder when Ms. Le-Fleur was just a young girl.

"Yes," I said, while I thought I had even heard the extended version thanks to Ernie.

"Then you know that her Uncle Sal and Aunt Stella came to Boca Vista and raised Ms. Le-Fleur as if she was their own daughter," Bruce said.

"Yes," I said, for lack of a better response.

"What you don't know is that Uncle Sal, over the years, took the business in a different direction …" He paused here so I could put two and two together.

"It has become a very profitable and legitimate business," Bruce said.

After what seemed like a long, pregnant pause he continued. "With Uncle Sal's health problems and Dominic's abrupt return, Ms. Le-Fleur began to experience dreadful flashbacks of the time her father was murdered. She was very young, but the fear that only a young child could experience when both her parents are taken from her has resurfaced in these flashbacks."

I looked over at Babbs who remained as motionless

as a statue, still staring out at *Pirate Life* as if she had mentally removed herself to the deck of the yacht for the telling of this story by Bruce.

"Ms. Le-Fleur confided in Charlie about her fears, and after some soul-searching, both she and Charlie concluded that what she was feeling was the real fear that the grocery business, like her father before her, was about to be taken away from her. She was listening to her instincts, which were telling her that Dominic was intent on not only taking over the grocery business but also taking it some steps backward if you know what I mean," he said.

"Yes, I think I do," I said.

"That is why it is imperative that Charlie is located to put a stop to this," the Queen now spoke. "My dear, I am no match for my nephew Dominic and his plans to take the grocery business in that backward direction."

"Ok," I said. "I understand, I really do," I said.

"There is something else you need to know," she said and turned to Bruce.

I watched while Bruce picked up and opened the cash purse she brought to our meeting today. Oh no, I thought, but this time he wasn't going to place more cash on my desk.

I watched while he retrieved an envelope out of the Queen's purse and handed it to me. I glanced down at it, opened it and took out a piece of paper. It was a

Google map with a handwritten note, which said, "8:00 pm – pick up."

I looked at the paper again and then looked back up at Bruce and the Queen for further explanation. I didn't have to wait long because the Queen resumed her staring at *Pirate Life* and Bruce continued.

"After Ms. Le-Fleur and Charlie spoke, the private investigator, Harry West, was hired to find out if her fears were valid and to take steps to prevent Dominic from taking over the grocery business. In fact, it was Mr. West who found this map and gave it to Ms. Le-Fleur at their last meeting.

"At that meeting, Mr. West told Ms. Le-Fleur that he met with Charlie before he left on his post tax season vacation and delivered a briefcase to Charlie. Mr. West had been following Dominic. The pickup was a briefcase. It contained cash which he suspected Dominic agreed to launder.

"Mr. West followed Dominic that night and watched as he left the briefcase in the trunk of his car and went into the mansion. It was dark, and he, let's just say, retrieved the briefcase and delivered it to Charlie. A few weeks later, as you now know, Mr. West was found murdered."

Bruce paused here to give me a minute to take in what he had just told me. I was quickly putting two and two together, at least the part about the briefcase, which I knew was now sitting in Jennifer's safe room.

"Do you know where the briefcase is now?" I asked.

"No," the Queen responded, now Bruce remained silent.

"Charlie told me he placed it in a secure location. I didn't ask where, and shortly afterward, he left on his fishing trip, and not long after that Mr. West was murdered. The rest you know," the Queen finished up the story, and with that, the meeting was over.

As they were leaving, and Bruce was holding the door for the Queen, just like Jennifer the other day, I got up and walked over to Bruce. I could see Babbs was now in the front chatting with Velma.

I turned to Bruce and said, "So the bottom line is she thinks the reason Dominic is back is because he plans to use the grocery business to launder money for the mob?"

"Well, actually no," Bruce said. "It seems, at least according to Mr. Rusky, the mob, just like the rest of corporate America, is sitting on their cash."

"Oh, so who is he in bed with?" I asked.

"Well that, my dear, is what she is hoping you figure out soon, but it may not be the mob," Bruce said.

"Well if it's not the mob, who could it be?" I asked Bruce like he would know the answer. Like Velma, he knew everything going on and then some.

He just looked at me and once again leaned closer

and removed some invisible lint from my suit jacket and said, "I don't know—terrorists maybe?" and he locked eyes with me for a split second and then followed Babbs right out the front door.

Velma and I watched as the Rolls took off. There it was, just like the other day, I was thinking, but instead of Babbs and Jennifer dropping the bomb, it was Babbs and Bruce. Terrorists, I thought. That would explain Ernie's interest.

I headed back to my office as Velma followed and I told her what I had heard during the meeting with Bruce and Queen Babbs. "I warned you," was all she said and then went back up to her command station.

Well, for now, I was at a standstill until I heard back from Boris and his family members about the fishing in Costa Rica. My regular work was piling up on my desk, so I decided to get back to work and sit tight and wait. Maybe the storm would blow over, but unfortunately, it was the beginning of hurricane season.

CHAPTER 17

The core Green Team consisted of four members. At any time, the team could expand to carry out their missions, but the core always remained. The team leader, known as Black Snake, was in complete command and controlled the movements of the team during their missions.

The four team members were in this for life; and due to the nature of their missions, had no life outside of the team and this suited them just fine. They lived for the mission and were happiest in the thick of battle. Their skills were unique, and the four core members of the Green Team were at the top of the food chain in the world of covert operators.

I guess you could say they were each ranked in the top ten of covert operators. That was why, after 9/11, these four were chosen to carry out the most important covert operations ensuring that another 9/11 would never happen again on U.S. soil.

But, time had passed and so had the memory of 9/11. It began to dim in the minds of the citizens of the U.S. as other things took priority, like the ups and downs of gas prices, foreclosures of their homes and the loss of their jobs.

The Green Team was so good at what they did that they pretty much covertly operated themselves out of a job with the U.S. government. After a few years, their missions were few and far between. They became similar to the Maytag man and had been placed on retainer with the feds. This all led to a lot of downtime, which led to boredom, and so, to escape boredom, Black Snake began to look for work elsewhere.

He would check in periodically with the defense contractors who had kept him and his team busy in the past. One contractor in particular was Jack Spoto. Jack headed one of the largest defense contractor operations in the U.S. It was headquartered in Cocoa Beach, Florida.

It also didn't hurt that Jack had the DOJ head of counter terrorism, Walther Roosevelt, on his side. Walther Roosevelt was an idealist and viewed himself as a savior of the free world. He knew Walther on a personal basis since he reported to Walther in his position with the feds and as the head of the Green Team. Contacts with Walther had dwindled lately.

Black Snake began to hear rumors that they could be facing the loss of their biggest client: the U.S. government. As it turned out, Jack, Walther and certain individuals high up the food chain in the current administration were also nervous about their cushy positions.

Sometime in the dead of a cold winter night, it was decided by Black Snake's superiors, Walther and his best bud Jack, that it was time for Americans to be reminded of the ever-present danger of a terrorist attack on U.S. soil. If nothing else, it would take their minds off the economy and the price of gas at the pumps.

So, a secret plan was hatched by Walther, with the help of Jack, to execute a terrorist attack on a prized symbol of America, a reminder of 9/11.

Since they didn't have any terrorists on hand to do the job for them, they decided that the Green Team would carry out the attack on the prized symbol. It was presented to Black Snake as a military exercise for the Green Team, which was common lately since no real terrorist attacks were taking place.

Jack would supply the cash for the operation so it couldn't be traced back to the feds. Ready money would come from his cash stash from the Save America PAC; after all, it was in line with the mission of the PAC. Black Snake knew something was up when Walther summoned him for a meeting at their covert meeting place *To the Moon Alice*, a bar in Cocoa Beach, which had been around since the early days of the space missions.

As they sat, surrounded by pictures of astronauts long gone, like the glory days of NASA, it was almost fitting that Walther explain the mission to Black Snake in this setting. NASA, like the war on terror, was fading.

So Walther sat with Black Snake and discussed the military exercise for the Green Team, but only Black Snake would be privy to the fact that this was not an exercise, and that it would be what Walther called a "real time exercise." It would involve a terrorist attack to blow up the Statue of Liberty. The operation would be called "Wake-Up America" and the "Queen of Freedom" would be the code name for the Statue of Liberty.

"Now you might have to do a little damage to the Queen of Freedom," Walther was saying to Black Snake. "Like blow off part of her crown. Nothing major," he cautioned. "Do you understand?"

Walther paused to make sure that Black Snake had understood that the damage would be superficial to the Statue of Liberty.

Black Snake nodded his understanding and then said, "It should not be difficult to plant a small explosive in the crown of the Queen of Freedom and detonate it from afar."

Walther continued, "Nothing major, of course, and nothing that won't be fixed immediately because our friends at the media will trigger a plea to the public for donations. We will move the team to NYC to a temporary command station and set you up there."

Walther stopped for a minute and seemed to gaze into his future while he explained his brilliant plot to Black Snake.

"The money will pour in along with lots of opportunities for aging rockers to hold concerts, just like they did right after 9/11," he said. "She needs an update anyway, and with all the budget cuts this will bring in the funds to take care of that project," Walther said while he finished his drink and looked up at a picture of a famous astronaut.

"Wake up, America," Walther said to the picture and lifted his empty drink glass in a toast to the long forgotten astronaut.

"Look what has happened to the space program," he said to the picture and took another swig from his empty glass.

Walther had always been a light drinker, Black Snake thought, which was good for him since he always told Black Snake more than he needed to know at these meetings.

"Who knows, maybe after this we will plot to blow up another symbol and bring in the money to refurbish it," Walther finished and ordered another round of drinks.

Black Snake just listened to Walther, who was obviously on a roll and rationalizing big-time about what he was suggesting.

"This is brilliant, Walther," Black Snake said, as he took a sip of his water and watched as Walther gulped down half his drink. It was brilliant, and Black Snake was already thinking ahead to the logistics and how to plan this with the other three team members.

The second in command on the Green Team was an operative known as Dirt Devil. He got that name because he was the navigator, the one who was sent ahead to sneak into enemy territory, and then just as quickly would sneak out, laying out the path into battle.

Dirt Devil took orders directly from Black Snake and was privy to information that the other two team members were not because the two others were not that bright. They were the dark ones, two brothers known in covert circles as Whacked Out and Wacko. They carried out the darker side of the missions, and if necessary, were willing to sacrifice their lives.

Walther, now blitzed because Black Snake made sure the drinks were strong and contained a little something to loosen his tongue, freely told him the cash would come from Jack Spoto.

Black Snake listened intently to this twist because he knew the more moving parts you added to an operation the more chances it could go wrong.

"We have tapped Ernie for the job in the field," Walther said. This was no surprise to Black Snake. He knew who Ernie was and that he was semi-retired, but his skills were invaluable, so he was called back into action from time to time. He had never met Ernie, but he knew all about Ernie and his partner, Rodeo. They were legendary in their own right.

Black Snake interrupted, "You think this is wise? Ernie may figure this out, and it could blow up in our faces," he said to Walther.

"I have thought about that, but it will all happen so

quick Ernie won't have time to figure it out. He will think he is looking for the terrorists threatening a national symbol. It's a chance we will have to take," Walther said.

Black Snake drove Walther back to his hotel that night and smiled while he thought about this brilliant plan of Walther's.

Black Snake made plans to skim some of the cash out of the secret operation just in case a speedy and comfy government retirement was needed if the operation fell through and he lost his job. Of course, the other three Green Team members won't have a clue and will accept it as they always had: a mission undertaken for the greater good. Amazing, Black Snake thought, how so much history had taken place for the greater good.

CHAPTER 18

The next couple of days went by quickly working on a couple of my clients' cases who were facing IRS audits. I had put Charlie and the rest of the drama out of my mind and was trying to give it a good rest while waiting to hear back from Boris about Charlie and Costa Rica. Until I found Charlie, I wasn't going near Dominic. But, the drama was not going away, no matter how hard I tried.

Velma had walked in one morning and sat across from my desk much like Babbs and Jennifer not that long ago.

"I decided to talk to Rodeo and pick his brain and thanks to Boris and his extended family in Costa Rica, they think they have a lead on Charlie," Velma said.

"You did?" I said, and then added, "They do?"

"Yep," Velma said.

I just sat there and looked at Velma.

After a moment of silence, I said, "Okay, so where is Charlie?"

Velma leaned closer to my desk and said, "Charlie is in Costa Rica. He's been sitting in a jail cell."

"In jail?" I said.

I sat there for a minute taking this bit of information

into account before I said, "Rodeo told you this?"
Velma sat there with the beginning of the 'If I told you
I'd have to shoot you' look, and I was just about to
decide not to waste time waiting for a response from
her when she said, "Charlie is on his way back. Boris
and his family were able to negotiate his release, and he
should be back tonight. He will be staying with Ernie
on his houseboat," Velma said.

"It was Dominic who had Charlie arrested," she
said.

"*Oh, really?*"

I just sat there a little stunned, but not entirely
surprised and waited, just in case there was more, but
Velma just got up and said, "You're welcome," and
headed back up front.

Velma never ceased to amaze me.

It dawned on me that Velma was feeding me this
information, hook, line, and sinker, and I thought I was
the one going fishing. "Okay," I said to myself, after a
long minute taking in everything Velma had told me.
Dang, I thought.

Jeez, I was beginning to feel like I was talking to
Aunt Sophia as she was doing a card reading for me!

But what had actually happened was a heads up
from Velma. Sometime today I would probably get a
call from Boris to let me know about Charlie. What
next, I wondered? I decided to put that thought on hold

for now. I walked up front and looked at Velma. "Velma," I said.

"Yeah," she said.

"Be careful."

Velma just looked at me. I watched her for a few minutes. She was just sitting there, deep in thought, staring out the front store window.

She looked at me and said, "Yeah, you too."

CHAPTER 19

Aunt Sadie and Aunt Sophia and Aunt Anna arrived in New York City and checked into the grand old lady, the Waldorf Astoria, along with Harold and Molly. They were there to attend the annual public access television convention being held at the Waldorf.

Aunt Sophia, who took her role as a public access television producer very seriously, was in her element. As they were checking into the hotel, she was busy giving anyone in the lobby that was within earshot a history lesson about public access television.

"You know that there are only about 400 public access television channels now in the U.S. and only one remaining in the state of Florida. These stations were created to provide a free speech forum open to all without discrimination or favoritism based on content. As it is now, we pretty much are spoon-fed by one voice on regular TV channels, which are reporting the news of the day or what they consider news of the day," she would say to those listening. "We must remember that we are not spectators, but we all have a right to exercise our freedom of speech." At these moments Aunt Anna knew to stand next to her sister to help her off her soapbox, but usually, it was with a round of applause for Aunt Sophia.

Aunt Sadie somehow talked the hotel check-in people into upgrading them to a large penthouse suite, something about the family having worked at the Waldorf, so all five ended up sharing the suite. They were all excited and felt just like they were back in high school on a field trip. The group soon set up camp in the lobby bar, which also served as the hospitality center for the public access convention. They were there not so much to drink, but for the free happy hour food, the public access folks dispensed.

It also just happened to be a place where Whacked Out and Wacko frequented for drinks from time to time since the Green Team's temporary mission control for Operation Save America was right down the street. Before long, they fell under Aunt Anna and Aunt Sophia's spell and became part of the group.

Aunt Anna had a way of endearing people to her especially if they had any secret desire to be on TV, which, it so happened, these two numbskulls did. They were looking ahead and had their own ideas on retirement.

They were both hoping to parlay their covert training and skills into making it big on a reality TV show. They also felt pretty sure they could pick up work as stunt men in the movies.

They didn't know the difference between public access and regular TV, so they were quickly drawn into the circle after a couple of drinks. To their ears, public access TV sounded just like reality TV. When they found out that Aunt Sophia read cards that really sealed their alliance.

Whacked Out and Wacko were both superstitious, and, in their line of work, they had a real concern about not making it to retirement. Their biggest fear was whether or not they would be pushing up daisies next week in some boneyard. They never discounted card readers or fortune tellers. That had served them well, so far, since after all, they were still standing and breathing.

It didn't hurt that Aunt Anna and Aunt Sophia reminded them both a little of their own grandmothers, short and squat, tough, wearing old lady dresses with black pumps and black purses.

Ernie and Rodeo had decided to put the Green Team under surveillance and were aware of their routines, which so far, had been pretty regular. They knew the brothers frequented the Waldorf for drinks.

At first, they were surprised to see the aunts at the Waldorf and checked it out with MC, who told them they were in New York City to attend the public access TV convention. What they didn't expect was Whacked Out and Wacko becoming best pals with Aunt Anna and then becoming part of the group. They decided they would just let it play out and figured the aunts would be back in Fish Camp in a few days. Just to be safe, Rodeo decided to keep an eye on the feisty women knowing their reputation for getting into trouble.

Rodeo was sitting in a corner of the bar watching them. None of the aunts knew him, so there was no chance that they would recognize him. Either way, he was sure that Aunt Sadie had heard an earful about him from Velma over the years, so he decided to keep his distance, just the same.

He had planted some bugs in the bar, and from where he sat he could hear their conversation. His ears had perked up earlier when he detected that those two wanted Aunt Sophia to read their cards. He and Ernie discussed this turn of events.

If the Wacko brothers were to open up to Aunt Sophia, it might tell them where this plot to blow up a national treasure was going down. Unfortunately, they would have to get Aunt Sophia involved so she could guide them into opening up under the spell of the fortune teller during the card reading.

He and Ernie decided to wait until the session was actually set up with the Wacko brothers before Rodeo would speak with Sophia and Anna. About the third day of the convention, he overheard Aunt Sophia setting up the card reading for the next afternoon. The two brothers were anxious to hear the cards speak to them.

Rodeo decided he immediately needed to speak with the aunts and hatch a plan to get as much information as possible out of the Wacko brothers.

Rodeo, taking a direct approach with Aunt Sophia and Aunt Anna, knocked on their hotel door the next morning. After a minute, the door opened slightly, and a short, but large, black woman peered out the door with the chain lock still intact.

It was Velma's Aunt Sadie; she was wearing a red hat with black feathers, her dress was white with black polka dots, and she wore black patent pumps. She looked like a cross between a Dalmatian and a peacock. He flashed his biggest smile, but it didn't work on Aunt Sadie, who stood there hat and all and was staring him down like a Marine. He wasn't surprised since Velma had the same ability. In a split second, he was not the number one covert operator in the country, but a twelve-year-old back in Sunday school caught red-handed and facing the firing squad of his mother and her Ya-Ya sisters.

He heard his voice crack a little as he said, "Hello, ma'am, I was wondering if I could have a word with Miss Sophia?"

"Who the hell are you?" Aunt Sadie said, still staring at Rodeo, with no blink of the eye.

Rodeo reached into his pocket. At the same time, Aunt Sadie reached into her large sized bra and simultaneously drew a small Berretta as Rodeo flashed his credentials.

"How do I know those aren't fake?" Aunt Sadie said, pointing the Berretta at Rodeo.

"Ma'am, I assure you these are not fake, and if you wish I have a number you can call to confirm the authenticity of those credentials," Rodeo said, all the while keeping his eye on this formidable black woman who got the drop on him, with a Berretta pointed directly at him. Something that no one in his days as an operative had been able to accomplish and live to talk about.

"That won't be necessary." And with that, she closed the door after snatching his credentials, leaving Rodeo standing out in the hallway wondering what he was going to do next.

"Dang gummit," he said out loud, shocked, standing alone in the hallway. About the time he was getting ready to call MC, the door opened, and standing before him was an elderly gentleman with a bearing he recognized as one earned by years in the military.

"Come in, young man," he said. Harold handed Rodeo back his credentials as he entered the suite.

"I am General Harold McCormick retired, and I see from your credentials you are with Homeland Security, but from my experience, I gather you are deeper than that," Harold said with a wink.

Rodeo saluted Harold and then said, "It's an honor to meet you, General McCormick, sir."

He had not seen him before in the bar with Aunt Sophia and Aunt Anna. A woman he did recognize from the bar came to stand next to Harold and said, "Hello, my name is Molly," as she reached out and gave him a firm handshake.

Aunt Sadie came next and also reached out to shake his hand. "Sorry about that, but you can never be too sure who you are dealing with in New York City."

"Yes, ma'am," Rodeo said, while he held Aunt Sadie's hand for a split second longer.

"You know, young man, you look familiar," Aunt Sadie said now, a little closer to Rodeo.

"Yes, ma'am" was all Rodeo said, while he stared at Aunt Sadie. He saw that Velma and Aunt Sadie had the same beautiful but penetrating eyes.

Standing before him now was Aunt Anna, whom he had not met, but he knew all about her and her shenanigans from MC. He bowed to shake her hand, and as she looked up into his eyes while shaking his hand, he immediately smiled back into her eyes. It was as if he was saying hello to an old friend who shared good memories with him. He knew instantly that this woman was trouble, and at the same time irresistible. As he shook her hand, he felt like they were kindred spirits.

"My, what a tall, good-looking man you are," Aunt Anna said with a twinkle in her eye.

"Thank you, ma'am," Rodeo said and winked back at her.

"Anna," Sophia said, and Anna released the handshake with a nod of her head and a wink in the direction of Aunt Sophia.

Rodeo then turned to meet Aunt Sophia. In every group, he knew there was a leader (having dealt with many leaders over the years as a covert operator), but despite his background and training, he was not prepared for Aunt Sophia. It was like a pro playing tennis with a beginner; their game threw you off balance.

He sat across from Aunt Sophia after introductions. He decided he had no choice but to include the entire group in what he had to say. Rodeo began his explanation as to why it was important to get information out of Whacked Out and Wacko, about what they were doing in New York. He then explained that he thought this could be done during the card reading Aunt Sophia had scheduled with these two Green Team members. He finished it up with telling the group that this was a matter of national security and that there was concern that these two were part of a terrorist plot.

"I can't do that," Aunt Sophia said to Rodeo. "It would be unprofessional."

Rodeo couldn't believe what he was hearing. An ethics problem had arisen with a fortune teller. He was quiet as they stared at each other. Aunt Sophia did not flinch. He knew then and there he had a problem. She was not going to share any information that she acquired during a card reading. He quickly changed tactics and relaxed his military persona as well as posture.

He spent the next half hour laying out all his arguments for Aunt Sophia. He threw in the towel. She was not going to budge. Even Harold with his military training was not able to persuade Aunt Sophia to use the reading to get the information for Rodeo.

Aunt Anna was sitting next to him with a tray of Greek cookies and spanakopita. He couldn't believe he was carrying on this conversation with MC's Aunt Sophia with his mouth full of Greek food.

"You don't understand, young man, this is a gift from God, which was given to me and my sister before me, and it is used with reverence to help those who come for guidance. We do not do it for money, but, of course, we accept any gifts that come our way," Aunt Sophia added with a nod and a smile.

"I have listened to you and understand completely what you are asking, but you will have to get that information another way. I suggest you do it quickly, like a bunny. Here she paused and pointed her finger at Rodeo, "I think my niece MC is involved in this national security issue." Rodeo was quiet and did not flinch when she brought up MC.

"I see," she said with finality.

"Anna, give Mr. Rodeo some more spanakopita," and she smiled.

Rodeo knew it was useless; he was not going to get Sophia to bend the rules of fortune-telling. It was obviously an ethics problem with the fortune tellers and psychics of the world. "OK, well, would you at least agree to postpone your session with the two to buy us some time?" Rodeo said.

Aunt Sophia thought about this for a minute. She then said something to Aunt Anna in Greek. She was about to say something to Rodeo when Harold spoke up.

"Sophia, I think you should at least consider that and postpone the session with those two numbskulls."

Aunt Sophia finally spoke and said, "Okay, okay, all right, I'll postpone the session. I'll give them a call right now."

Rodeo's ears perked up.

"Wait a minute—you have their telephone number?"

"Well, yes—they gave it to me in case something came up."

"Will you be so kind as to give me the number?"

"I will, to keep my niece safe," she said as she showed Rodeo the number Whacko had written on the back of a paper napkin from the lobby bar in the Astoria.

"Can I have this napkin?"

Aunt Sophia hesitated for a minute and then sighed and said, "Fine," as she handed over the napkin to Rodeo.

Aunt Anna piped in, "DNA, huh? Maybe you can lift a good set of prints from the napkin?"

"Anna, this is not the crime channel. This is serious,"Aunt Sophia's psychic voice now spoke followed by a short but loud outburst between the two in Greek, as everyone sat and watched.

"Okay, okay," Anna finally said, and then gave a conspiratorial wink to Rodeo, who returned it with a wink of his own.

"Do you mind if I listen to the call?" Rodeo said to Aunt Sophia.

"Fine," Aunt Sophia repeated almost under her breath as she picked up her cell and dialed the number and then added, "Finish your spanakopita, it's from the best Greek deli in New York."

Rodeo listened, and all eyes were on Aunt Sophia as she rang the number.

"Seymour, this is Sophia. Yes, I am fine and you? Oh, I am sorry to hear that. Take some Vitamin C right away."

Rodeo felt his eyes wanting to roll back in his head. This woman had managed to connect with these two on a level where they felt comfortable letting their guards down, to the point she knew them by their real names. Usually, this took months to achieve, but Aunt Sophia had managed it in only a few days.

"Ah, something has come up, Seymour," Aunt

Sophia said and looked directly at Rodeo without batting an eye. "I need to postpone our session until tomorrow morning," Aunt Sophia said while nodding her head up at Rodeo, who gave her the okay sign while he watched Aunt Sophia in disbelief as she wrapped up the call.

"Okay, so we will see you and Henry tomorrow at 11 am."

"Bye-bye," Aunt Sophia said. She clicked the cell off, calmly placed it in her black purse and snapped it closed.

"Well, does that satisfy you?" Aunt Sophia asked.

"Henry?" Rodeo asked.

"Henry is Seymour's younger brother," and then she leaned a little closer to Rodeo saying, "Not all up there" and pointed her finger at the side of her forehead.

'Not all up there' was an understatement, Rodeo thought, taking that to understand that Henry was the member of the team known as Whacked Out.

With that, Rodeo got up and gave Aunt Sophia a big hug, as well as Aunt Anna and Molly, and saluted Harold as he started heading toward the door.

Aunt Sadie followed him, reached out and took his hands, "You be careful, young man," she said, and her eyes looked directly into his soul.

"Yes ma'am, I will," he said as he held her hands for a second longer. He stepped out, and she closed the door.

He would call Ernie and bring him up to speed and post a team of men to make sure no harm came to this group, especially Aunt Sadie. He could never live with that.

CHAPTER 20

MC had been trying for most of the morning to get hold of her aunts on their cell phone to check on them. Dang, she thought, getting her Aunt Sophia's voice mail again. She had told them at least a hundred times, when going over the operation of their cell, to keep the phone on. It drove her crazy. She had just put down her cell when the office phone rang.

Velma picked it up and then buzzed her.

"It's Ernie," Velma said.

"Do you know what he wants?" I asked, not really wanting to talk with him anymore. As far as I was concerned, he was the grim reaper. After Velma and I had talked, that afternoon Boris had sent over a dozen roses with a note *package delivered safe and sound*. I figured the package was Charlie. So, I could lie low now and let the pieces fall where they may. As far as I was concerned, I had fulfilled my part in this drama and was back on track with my life as a tax accountant.

"No," Velma said, "but he said he needs to talk to you, and it's urgent."

"It's always urgent with him," I grumbled and reluctantly picked up the phone.

"What's up?" I said to Ernie, as Velma walked into the office and sat down.

"MC."

"Yes."

"We need you and Velma in New York City."

"New York City?" I felt a chill run down my back.

I gripped the phone tighter now. All I could think about was Aunt Sophia and Aunt Anna in New York City.

"Aunt Sophia and Aunt Anna—are they all right?" I asked holding my breath with my eyes closed.

"All right?" I heard Ernie say. "Yes, your aunts are more than all right, they're a handful, and that's why I need you and Velma in New York City—to rein them and Velma's Aunt Sadie in."

I opened my eyes and bolted out of my chair.

"What do you mean, "rein them in?"" I said, as I looked up at Velma, who had her 'what's up?' expression on her face.

"Wait a minute," I said. "I want to put you on speakerphone so Velma can hear this also."

"Are you ready?" Ernie said. His voice, even and controlled, and now heard by Velma, who leaned closer to the phone despite the fact that his voice was heard by the both of us, loud and clear.

"Your three aunts are fine, and so is their whole TV crew. In fact, MC, your Aunt Sophia has managed to do something our best operatives would have taken years to do – she has infiltrated the Green Team."

I collapsed into my chair, and Velma threw her hands up in the air.

"Somehow, MC, your Aunt Sophia, with the help of your Aunt Anna, and your Aunt Sadie, Velma, got two cockamamie robots, named Whacked Out and Wacko, to confide in and trust them."

Velma and I just looked at each other, and I'm sure neither of us really wanted to hear the rest of the story.

"What?" I said, feeling my back tense up along with my jaw. "What do you mean they got two members of the Green Team to confide in them? Who the hell are they and how the hell did they do that?" I asked at the same time recalling my conversation with Rodeo when he shared this information, and I swore to keep it secret.

As I sat there taking a deep breath, I closed my eyes, and then I opened them I could see Izzy strolling into the office.

"Oh brother," I said to myself.

Ernie paused for a second and then continued.

"The Green Team are four freelance covert operatives, highly skilled. Whacked Out and Wacko are two brothers and are intrigued with your Aunt Sophia's ability to read the fortune-telling cards, and your aunt has managed to get them to drop their guard with the promise of a reading and the possibility of a role on their TV show."

I almost jumped out of the chair as I felt my jaw tense. I bit my tongue.

"Shut the front door," I said.

"I don't like their names," Velma chimed in, "Whacked Out and Wacko."

Ernie, not paying any attention, continued, "Oh, there's more – as if your Aunt Sophia and Aunt Anna aren't enough, Velma's Aunt Sadie managed to get the drop on Rodeo – something that has never been done in all his years as an operative. Rodeo is at the top of his game. It blew his mind."

Now it was Velma's turn to jump out of the chair. "Shut the back door," she said. And then, at an octave high enough to cause Izzy to jump, turn and scurry out of the office, she asked, "Rodeo? Rodeo was talking to my Aunt Sadie? What were they talking about Ernie, do you know?"

"Look, you two, I don't have time to get into all the details. I'll bring you both up to speed when you get to New York City. Just know that we need both of you here because you two are the only ones who have any influence over your aunts. We are just hoping they will listen to you both because, like it or not, they have all become central players in a matter of utmost security to the nation. The president has been informed of the latest events," Ernie said.

"The president?" we both said in unison. "Really."

I sat there not believing what I was hearing. On the one hand, I was relieved that my aunts were safe but, on the other hand, my fear was now replaced with a well-known annoyance, which I knew was the result of my inability to control my aunts any more than I could control my mother before them. I was the queen of control freaks, second to none except maybe Velma, and it did not look like she had any control over her Aunt Sadie at the moment.

"Okay," I said to Ernie, resigning myself to whatever was next. I just needed to see this whole mess to the end. "How do we get to New York?" Are we going to be beamed up? I silently thought.

"You and Velma each pack a light bag and someone will contact you both to transport you via military helicopter to Manhattan. We have a room for you both at the same hotel your aunts are staying at. We'll talk when I see you this evening," and then he hung up.

"I need to know what Aunt Sadie and Rodeo were talking about," Velma said as if she didn't hear any of the conversation and the fact that we were going to be transported to New York City probably via a Blackhawk helicopter for a matter that involved national security and now our three aunts.

We probably were going to see them on the evening news next, and Velma was interested in what went on between Rodeo and her Aunt Sadie. "Velma," I said, "Is there something about you and Rodeo that I don't know? If there is, it might be time to let me in because it might mean our backs. Did you not hear any of Ernie's conversation?"

"You're damn right there is," and she marched out of the office and gathered her stuff. As she was slamming the front door, she said, "I'll see you shortly. We got a helicopter to catch. Leave Izzy some water and food and kitty litter for his box," and out the door, she went.

I went up front and just stared down at Izzy.

"Right now, I wish you could talk," I said looking down at Izzy, "but it's probably just as well that you can't, or you could wind up as lizard meat."

Izzy just looked up at me, and for a second I actually thought I could hear him, or maybe he was going to sign language me with his little, webbed feet; instead, he took that as a cue to scurry under Velma's desk. Dang, and we hadn't even had our training on how to shoot!

CHAPTER 21

I had just turned off my computer, so I could run home and pack to go to New York when the front office door opened. Figuring it was Velma, I was just about to say something, when I heard, "Hello, MC."

As I looked up, I caught my breath because standing in the doorway to my office was a ghost named Charlie Le-Fleur.

He stood there as if he had just been in the neighborhood and was dropping by to say hello. He had a big old grin on his tanned, handsome face. "Mind if I sit down?" Still smiling, he walked into my office and sat down in the same chair his wife had occupied not too long ago.

"Please," I said, regaining my composure from somewhere. "Make yourself at home and tell me what you've been up to Charlie. By the way, your wife was by with a client of yours, Jennifer Stone," I looked at the clock in my office. *I'm sure the helicopter will wait. I had to hear this.*

He just sat there with a big old charming grin on his face that reminded me of the Cheshire Cat. "They engaged me in a game of hide and seek," I said. The grin disappeared and, in its place, was a deep sigh. "MC, I don't have much time, but I do apologize for what has landed you in the middle of a family squabble."

"Family squabble?" I exclaimed. "Well, the family *squabble* has so far left one man dead and landed you in a Costa Rican jail. By the way, have you spoken to Babbs? Does she know you've returned from the dead?"

"Actually, no. That is what I want to talk to you about," Charlie said.

I couldn't believe what I was hearing. I just sat there growing numb as I looked across the desk at Charlie Le-Fleur all decked out in a colorful resort shirt and shorts and Sperry Top-Sider shoes. He looked like he had just stepped off of *Pirate Life*.

Right then, I was hoping he would step back on it and depart. I had that helicopter to catch. But, a little voice in my head told me that something he was about to tell me would tie into this trip to New York.

"Dominic killed Harry West," Charlie said right off the bat.

"He also arranged for what could have turned out to be an extended stay in that Costa Rican jail if it hadn't been for you and Boris," Charlie continued. He got up and was now looking out the office window.

"Is that *Pirate Life?*" he asked.

"Yep," I said.

"Hmm, I think I know the owner."

No surprise there, I thought, as he turned back to look at me and continue his explanation of where he had been the last couple of months.

"My last meeting with Harry West came with a bit of a surprise. He handed over a suitcase full of cash and told me to put it somewhere safe. He had managed to separate it from Dominic, whom he had followed back from a meeting where he'd picked up the cash," Charlie said rather incredulously.

"Do you believe that? What an arrogant imbecile," Charlie continued, while he got up. I watched him as he continued to look out the window at *Pirate Life*.

"Yeah, I know the owner of that baby," Charlie said.

I just sat there with my eyes closed while I was saying silent prayers to Saint Anthony. *Please, Saint Anthony, wake me up from this nightmare.* I opened my eyes, and unfortunately, Charlie was still there.

"Harry West directed me to hide the briefcase of cash. So, I did. And then, also as directed by Harry West, I reluctantly took off on my post tax season fishing trip. I argued with him about leaving, but he said he didn't want any changes in routine that might alert Dominic. Harry also thought that Dominic would probably think I took the cash and come looking for me. He never got a chance to tell me the rest of the plan." Charlie stopped for a second, while he stared out at *Pirate Life*. "Stay away from the owner of *Pirate Life*, MC," Charlie said.

"Okay," I replied while rolling my eyes with a deep

sigh.

Charlie just watched for a minute and then went on with his story.

"Harry did suggest that for safety's sake, I go somewhere different than the Keys for my fishing trip. I had been to Costa Rica before, so instead of the Keys I took off for Costa Rica," he said.

"Wait a minute," I said. "Did Babbs know you went to Costa Rica instead of the Keys?"

"No," Charlie said with his eyebrows furrowed and his lips in a tight straight line. "Harry didn't want Babbs to know. He thought it would put her in harm's way, but I wasn't going to take off and not let anyone know, so I let Bruce know that I went to Costa Rica instead of the Keys."

I just looked directly at Charlie, closed my eyes and shook my head for a moment. *Bruce? Why wasn't I surprised?* Charlie went on.

"I have no doubt that what happened next was that Dominic killed Harry West. But, clearly, he got neither my location nor the location of the cash out of him before doing so," Charlie said, and then almost in a whisper, "Otherwise, I'd be dead and so would Jennifer, for that matter."

I sat there now thinking that one all the way through while I glanced over in the direction of *Pirate Life*. He was right, I thought. Charlie and Jennifer would have both become expendable at that moment.

"I also have no doubt, though, that he tracked me down with the help of some of his associates, and had me arrested and thrown in jail in Costa Rica," Charlie said.

"Really?" I said. "How do you know that?"

"I know because the sorry excuse for a human being paid me a visit while I was sitting in jail. He wanted to know where the cash was, and he told me if I didn't tell him I'd be spending the rest of my life in jail in Costa Rica. But, if I cooperated, I could join him in his new venture, and we all could make millions in the grocery business."

"What did you say?" I asked.

"I refused," Charlie said. He reached both arms up for a stretch. Probably thinking about that jail cell in Costa Rica I thought.

"MC," he said, still looking out the window at the water and docks, "I will tell you this. Dominic is not the sharpest tack in the tool box, but because he is so stupid, he is very dangerous." Charlie walked back and was standing behind the chair looking at me almost like Babbs did not too long ago.

"So, he said, fine. Sit in jail for a while, and think about it. But when I come back, you and I are going on a little trip to pick up that cash," Charlie said with real anger in his voice.

"Since I've been back, I've been lying low on Ernie's houseboat. Dominic has his men out looking for me and for the cash, which he needs back, or he will be on life support. Bruce has been watching Dominic, as you know, for some time now, and he came across something very interesting."

"You mean like Boris Rusky's cookbooks?" I asked.

Charlie just smiled at me with one of his famous smiles and pointed his pointer finger at me. Then he got real serious.

"MC, here is what you need to know. Dominic is going back into the laundry business like his namesake, Babbs's father. But not with any family members," he said while looking at me with the 'Velma pay attention I'm about to tell you something important' look. So, I did.

"He is going into business with a group that has ties to terrorists," Charlie said and gave me a minute to take this in, which I did like a drowning person.

"I have proof of this," Charlie said, and then he reached into his shirt pocket and held up a small, black flash drive like it was a prize!

I just looked at it like it was going to say something being the computer dork I am.

"What is that thing?" I asked. "This thing is a flash drive, and it has proof that Dominic is going into business with some bad guys and plans to use the grocery business to launder their money," Charlie said.

"It is? Where did you get that?"

"Harry West gave it to me when he delivered the cash. It contains pictures of Dominic at a meeting with the terrorists where they handed over the cash to him. This flash drive has been sitting safely on Ernie's houseboat. I asked Ernie to take a look at it before I left for Costa Rica."

"It was Ernie who discovered that Dominic and his group had ties to terrorists," Charlie said. *Ernie! Score one for the little voice.*

I'm not sure where what happened next came from. Maybe it was that Charlie was still standing, and it looked like he was about to wrap up our little chat and head out the door. Maybe it was the little voice in my head hollering out my ears, or my guardian angel that deserves a big raise.

But thinking back, the voice in my head sounded a lot like my mother's, and before I knew it, I heard myself blurt out, "Wait a minute. You're not going to tell me next that Dominic has something to do with this plot to blow something up that is a historical, patriotic symbol located somewhere in the U.S. Are you? The one I'm about to find out more about, since somehow my aunts and Velma's Aunt Sadie are now best buds with two freelance covert operators who, according to our mutual friend Ernie, may be part of a plot to blow up a national treasure?"

Charlie just looked at me, sat down and then said, "Explain please."

So, I did. It felt good to tell Charlie, and somehow it felt right. Just that gut feeling you get when you know you made the right decision.

After I had brought him up to speed, he sat there for the longest time staring into a place I did not know and then said, "I need something to drink." I got out the bottle of ouzo and handed him a red solo cup. He poured himself a shot, got up and stared out at *Pirate Life*, drank up and then came back. We resumed our conversation. "Well, MC, I think we can kill two birds with one stone."

"We can?" I said.

"What I have in mind is a way out of this mess for you, me and Babbs, and at the same time get rid of Dominic."

"What did you have in mind?"

"I think we should get Dominic to come to New York on the premise that I will have his cash waiting for him."

"We should?" I said. "Why should we do that?"

"Because then Ernie can nab him for both terrorism *and* the murder of Harry West," Charlie said.

With that, he got up, walked over and gave me a

kiss on the cheek, "For old times," he said and started to walk out the door.

"Wait a minute."

Charlie turned back and said,

"MC, you know I'm a married man now." I gave him the evil eye and said, "Yes, I'm aware of that having met your wife. No, I was going to say, 'what about Ernie'?"

"I'll give him a call."

"You will?" I asked.

"And, I'll see you in New York," he said as his cell rang. He answered his cell and said, "Just a minute," and looked back at me. "Speak of the devil, it's Ernie. I'll bring him up to speed," he whispered to me with a wink. "You better get going sweetheart. You have a chopper to catch." And he walked out of my office. I stood up front with Izzy and watched Charlie get in the Royal Rolls with Bruce.

"Shut the front door, Izzy, and the back door too. Will this ever end?"

CHAPTER 22

Velma and I were escorted aboard a military helicopter by men in black uniforms and whisked to Manhattan, where we found ourselves in the middle of our worst nightmares, only we were awake. We were now in the hotel suite along with our respective aunts and Ernie, who was in full-blown operative mode.

While on the chopper, I had brought Velma up to date on my visit from Charlie. Oddly, she didn't seem to be all that surprised and was more concerned about leaving food for Izzy. I gathered she had been speaking with Rodeo, who had kept her in the loop for reasons neither one had shared with me. But, it was becoming pretty clear to me that they had a connection. My guess was that it was those two beautiful twin girls.

"Ladies, we need to talk, and we don't have a lot of time," Ernie said to Velma and me, while our aunts sat on a sofa and chairs talking about their public access shows.

They seemed oblivious to what was going on around them as if it was all a movie and they had starring roles. All except for my Aunt Sophia who stared out the window deep in thought.

Ernie directed us over to a corner in the suite. I was growing numb from all the drama. It seemed as if it was a lifetime ago when I had spent my days in the safety of my office and my life as a small-town tax accountant.

Now, not only I but Velma and our aunts were all part of this crazy situation. I was hoping the nightmare would end soon so we could get back to our normal lives, whatever that meant. Unfortunately, it was about to get worse; we heard a knock at the door.

Ernie said to the both of us, "Wait here," and we watched while he went over and opened the door to the suite. In walked Jennifer and Charlie followed by Rodeo.

Charlie was still dressed like he had just stepped off a sixty-foot Hatteras sport fishing boat, except for the briefcase in his hand. And, since Jennifer was joining us, I was sure it was the one he had dropped off at Jennifer's house for safekeeping before his extended fishing trip in Costa Rica.

Jennifer looked around the room while Ernie said, "Jennifer, please have a seat."

Aunt Anna scooted over and patted the sofa to let Jennifer know she should sit next to her and gave her a hug and a big smile like we were all at a party. *Jennifer* looked at me with a 'so what is going on now' expression, while I just stared at Charlie, who remained standing and looked at me with that big grin on his face.

I looked at Velma, who was giving Rodeo the evil eye. This wasn't a nightmare, it was something straight out of the Twilight Zone.

Ernie returned to Velma and me and said, "We now know that Dominic is somehow tied into this plot.

"And, we are pretty sure we know the location, It's the Statue of Liberty," he said.

"The Statue of Liberty?" Velma asked.

"The Statue of Liberty!" I echoed.

"Yes," Ernie said and stared at us both for a second.

"Yes," he said, "the Statue of Liberty." He continued while we held our breaths.

"Harry West gave Charlie a flash drive full of pictures along with a briefcase full of cash which Charlie parked at Jennifer's."

We just listened and continued to hold our breaths.

"It showed Dominic meeting with a group that we know has ties to terrorists. We believe that the purpose of that meeting was to set up a money laundering scheme using Babbs's grocery business. What's new that Charlie just told us, in the last few hours, is that Bruce was keeping his eye on Dominic, and one day overheard a strange telephone conversation. Dominic was talking to someone about coordinating the funds for a plot to blow up a national treasure. We now know that it was a terrorist group Dominic was speaking to. Quite a coincidence, don't you think?" Ernie said, looking straight at Velma and me.

"Yeah," Velma said while looking at me, "a real coincidence."

I just looked at Charlie, who had been watching us intently since he arrived. He was standing next to

Rodeo, who was standing at attention, also in full operative mode.

Ernie just stared at the both of us for what was the longest second and then led Velma and me over to the sofa and chairs to have a seat. I looked over at Aunt Anna, who reached over with a big smile and patted my knee while I gave her my most serious stare down but to no avail.

Aunt Sophia was still looking very solemn, and while she gave Aunt Anna the evil eye, she leaned over and whispered in my ear, "We need to talk." Jennifer was now looking a little bored, and what I gathered from the look she was giving me, a little steamed that no one had clued her in on what was going on in this room.

It looked like Charlie was about to address the group, and I knew he was about to spin a tale, part fiction, and part nonfiction, but mostly true. He was going to spin this to get Dominic permanently out of the picture for Babbs, and I had a feeling Ernie was going along because of the murderer of his warrior friend, Harry West.

Charlie began the story."First let me say how sorry I am to Aunt Sophia, Aunt Anna and Aunt Sadie for finding yourselves in the middle of what started as a family matter between my wife Babbs and her nephew Dominic," Charlie said with all his southern gentlemanly charm.

I watched as Aunt Anna smiled back at him, Aunt Sadie stared back as cool as a cucumber, and Aunt Sophia, as you would have thought, gave him the evil eye.

"I was as surprised as you at what I am about to tell you. When I discovered that Dominic was involved with terrorists. He returned to Boca Vista when his father, Sal, became ill. Apparently, he decided to stay and turn the family's thriving, legitimate grocery business into a financial laundromat," Charlie said, showing genuine anger.

I just sat there with Velma watching the group as they were mesmerized by Charlie, who was always good at this type of thing. I gave Velma a look, and she looked back at me because we had already guessed where he was going. Charlie was going to spin this so that Dominic was part of this plot to take down a national treasure. Dang, I thought. Charlie was setting up Dominic to protect Babbs, and he hoped Ernie would go for it because he was out to avenge his friend and fellow Marine, Harry West.

"Right before I was to head out on my annual post tax season fishing trip, Babbs and I had a talk about Dominic. Babbs had been suspicious for some time that Dominic was just cooling his heels waiting for the opportunity to take over the family business when his father, Sal, was either dead or no longer able to run the business. It was rapidly becoming clear to her that Dominic had plans to go into partnership with what she thought at the time was the mob and use the grocery business to launder cash." Charlie moved a little closer to the group and continued.

"Babbs had already put two and two together, partly by sending her personal assistant, Bruce, on missions to spy on Dominic. But it was only confirmed after she hired the private detective, Harry West, to get to the bottom of this," he said.

"She was livid about it, and she also told me that she was beginning to have flashbacks about her father's murder, which happened when she was very young and shortly after her mother had died. The memories had been triggered by Uncle Sal's failing health, and then the threat of Dominic going back into business with the mob intensified them."

Charlie now had everyone's attention.

"Let me tell you that she just wasn't about to let the mob take over the business again, especially if they had anything to do with her father's murder. Even if that meant she was placed in harm's way by Dominic, which she was after Harry West was murdered."

"I got word to Babbs and suggested that you three have your meeting," Ernie interjected and broke the spell Charlie had cast on us.

Charlie continued. "I now know it was Dominic who ordered the hit on Harry West. He had also arranged to have me jailed in Costa Rica and warned me that a similar fate would come to both Babbs and me if we didn't come on board with his plans for the grocery business. What I hadn't yet discovered until after my return from Costa Rica, was that the group of terrorists that Dominic intends to go into business with is the same group of terrorists that were plotting to take down the Statue of Liberty." Wow, I thought. That was a leap of faith.

"How do you know that, young man?" Aunt Sophia asked.

Whoops, I thought. Charlie didn't know he was up against Aunt Sophia and her secret weapons of being psychic and the family fortune-telling cards.

About that time, I looked over at Ernie, and he sensed we had heard all we needed to hear. He stood up to take over the reins from Charlie and cut Aunt Sophia off at the pass.

"Aunt Sophia, that is an excellent question," Ernie said looking directly at Charlie. For your safety, and the safety of Aunt Anna and Aunt Sadie, we cannot reveal any more information than that.

"I hope you understand that we are working quickly to return the three of you to your homes and complete your part of this sordid matter, for which your country is most appreciative."

Aunt Sophia just gave Ernie the evil eye and then looked at me, but said no more. I'll have to talk with her later and see what was on her mind.

"But wait," I heard the echo whose name was Jennifer say, and then she looked directly at Charlie. I knew she was going to ask why she was involved in all this and why he left a load of cash in her safekeeping, putting her smack in the middle of this mess. Just then Charlie, the scoundrel, appeared.

"Jennifer, I am really sorry I involved you in this matter," he said. "I hope to make it up to you when it's all over."

Jennifer just looked at him and said, "Don't worry, you will."

I looked over at Rodeo, who was just standing at attention. Boy, there was more to this story than a soap opera.

"Okay, this is the plan, and unfortunately Aunt Sophia, Aunt Anna, and Aunt Sadie, you three must play a big part," I heard Ernie say as he took charge of the meeting.

I just looked at him with consternation when he said our aunts would play a big part. Then I looked over at Velma and saw a mirror reflection of my thoughts on her face. This was like opening Pandora's Box, and for the next half hour I listened to Ernie lay out the plan.

Aunt Sophia, Aunt Anna, and Aunt Sadie's parts were to hold off Whacked Out and Wacko by stalling them with some cockamamie story that the cards weren't talking that day, and they had to be patient. They were to invite them to join them back at their suite at the Waldorf for a little lunch, and keep them busy until the cards woke up.

Aunt Sophia agreed reluctantly to go along with the plan and to advise the brothers that it would be a good idea to postpone any major undertakings for the next few days until the cards spoke. She only did this because, apparently, she said to us in a very grave voice, "it was true."

Worse, Velma and I were given the part of watching Jennifer's back, while Jennifer was given the biggest acting role of her life, and her demeanor picked up when she heard her part.

Jennifer was to approach Black Snake and using all talents and feminine wiles, she was to play the role of damsel in distress using her unlimited charms to buy some time. Meanwhile, Rodeo would break into their office and see what he can find about the plot to blow up the Statue of Liberty and see if he could find evidence as Charlie suggested that it had a connection to Dominic.

So, he embellished the story a little, I thought. I could see the look on Charlie's face as he looked at me. Dominic was involved with terrorists, and this way he gets what's coming to him, and the murder of Harry West is avenged.

I wanted to shoot Charlie by the time they finished with all the details. Charlie walked over and very calmly whispered, "Don't worry about your aunts, they will be fine, and Jennifer is very good at what she has been asked to do. She has been playing that part all her life. Rodeo will be there in a second if anything goes wrong," he said.

"Okay, but how are you going to get Dominic to show up?" I asked.

He handed me the briefcase, which I could tell was empty. "I'm going to show him the money. He is on his way, as we speak."

"He is?"

"Yep, it will be over before you know it. And you, Jennifer, Velma and your aunts will be back at home having a big laugh over this adventure. But, it will be something you can all talk about for the rest of your days."

"Yeah, sure," I said.

I looked him straight in the eye and said, "If anything happens to our aunts, you will have something to talk about for the rest of your days because I'll see to it that my friend, Boris Rusky, who is in my debt since I returned his cookbooks, will return you to that jail in Costa Rica." With that, Charlie leaned over and gave me a kiss on the cheek. "Maybe someday we can all have shots of tequila and laugh about all this."

Yeah, we'll have shots of something, I thought as I watched him walk out the door with Rodeo.

Ernie had the last word. "Get your rest, and we will

all meet back here at eight a.m. sharp." He bid us good night, and he disappeared for the evening.

We all made a beeline for bed. We needed our rest since tomorrow morning the whole plan was to roll out. I was so exhausted I fell sound asleep as soon as my head hit the pillow.

I woke in the middle of the night and jumped for a second when I heard Velma snoring in the bed next to me. It wasn't a dream, after all. It was real. As I lay back down, I pulled the covers over my head.

## CHAPTER 23

Velma and I arrived at the Green Team's office building and watched Jennifer as she waited in the lobby. We were in the small gift shop and could see her from where we were standing.

Black Snake and Dirt Devil were out of their office, and Rodeo was up there looking for some proof about the plot to blow up the Statue of Liberty. According to Ernie, they were pretty predictable. They went to lunch about the same time each day and ate at the same place.

Rodeo was also in the building, and we had our cells so we could call when the bad guys returned and headed up to their office. I looked around and spotted some of Ernie's men in black, so we felt pretty safe. Jennifer was dressed in her best Hoochie Mama outfit and was gathering a lot of looks from men who stopped dead in their tracks. A few even were brave enough to try to spark up a conversation with her. Charlie was right; she had been playing this role all her life.

Whacked Out and Wacko were with Aunt Sophia waiting patiently for the cards to speak to them, while Aunt Anna stuffed them with Greek food, and Aunt Sadie kept them supplied with shots of ouzo.

Velma froze and dragged me to another side of the gift shop where we could see Jennifer and watch as two men walked into the building. One was tall and balding, but lean and well built. The other a shorter, younger version of the first. Jennifer had been given descriptions of Black Snake and Dirt Devil and managed to bump into them when they came into the building.

I looked at Velma and said, "Is that them? Do you know those two?"

"It's them," she said. "Black Snake and Dirt Devil, they are the other two members of the Green Team."

"Have you met them?" I asked Velma.

"Black Snake once, a long time ago, when we worked at the IRS, so I don't want him to see me. But, he's never seen you, so you need to go over there with Jennifer and keep them occupied while I call Rodeo. Keep the little party going until I give you a signal, then we can get Jennifer and get the hell out of here before they go up to their office."

Another Velma mystery, I didn't really want to go over there. From where I was, I could see that Jennifer looked like she was handling the situation just fine. They both were deep under the Jennifer spell.

Before I knew it, though, Velma pushed me out the door of the gift shop, and about the same time, Jennifer caught a glimpse of me.

"Suzy," she hollered at me. "Where have you been? I've been waiting for you."

I reluctantly made my way over to where she was standing with the two top dogs of the Green Team, who at a minute's notice, could shorten our lives right there in the lobby of the office building.

"Hey," I said, as I waited for her next line. She kept the conversation going for the next ten minutes. I don't think they heard a word she said, and I'm pretty sure they forgot I was even standing there after a few moments. I continued to look over at the gift shop from time to time waiting for Velma to give me the 'all clear' signal. I was getting worried, but finally, she appeared and gave me the 'okay you can leave now' signal.

"Come on, sweetie. We have a lot of shopping to do," I said to Jennifer. The two men looked at me with what I suspect was the Green Team's version of the evil eye. Jennifer gave her best pout and reached over and gave Black Snake a very close hug.

I saw his eyes glaze over, and it looked like Dirt Devil was going to pass out when she gave him a good-bye hug, too. There it was. Her power to cloud men's minds by propping up her girls. It didn't matter who they were because the reaction was always the same.

I grabbed her hand and ushered her out the door and looked back to see the two of them blowing kisses at Jennifer. We walked quickly about a half block down the street, and I breathed a sigh of relief when Velma appeared. Then we headed in the direction of the Waldorf Astoria.

Velma stayed a short distance behind us until we reached the hotel. Our instructions now were to wait in the bar until we heard from either Ernie or Rodeo that the coast was clear and that our aunts had finished with their two marks.

I ordered a stiff drink, even though it was early in the afternoon, to get me through the wait. I wanted nothing more than to hear that our aunts were safe and sound, and their part in this Broadway play was complete. As nice as it was, I was ready to check out of the Waldorf, hop on that military chopper, and return home safe and sound.

"You're having a drink?" Velma asked.

"Yes, I am," I said and added, "You got a problem with that? Let's just say this, between yesterday and what just happened, I could use a stiff drink."

Velma just looked at me and then said to the bartender, "Give me whatever she's drinking, and make it a double."

Jennifer ordered champagne instead. We both just looked at her in amazement. She excused herself to go powder her nose.

Taking an educated guess that Rodeo had found Velma and talked to her before she left the building after the drinks had calmed our jitters, I looked at her and said, "Did Rodeo find anything in their office?"

Velma took another sip of her drink, looked at me and said, "He told me that he didn't find anything other than confirmation of what they already knew and also one additional thing the two of them had suspected."

"What's that?" I asked.

"That they were operatives and worked under the direction of someone high up in the Department of Justice," Velma said and ordered another drink.

"Oh," I said and then out of that psychic side of my brain I avoided. "And would that be Walther Roosevelt?"

"Yep," Velma said looking at me for a second as we watched Jennifer making her way back to the bar. Then she decided it was okay to add, "They, Walther, and some big defense contractor by the name of Jack Spoto, are the ones behind the plot to blow up the Statue of Liberty."

"Really?" I said as I looked at her. She was now smiling at Jennifer making her way back to the bar.

Velma turned toward Jennifer and asked, "How did you know it was them, Jennifer?" Velma was looking at me very seriously, and smiling at Jennifer, while I still thought about what she just told me.

"I didn't. It was a hunch. Their looks matched the descriptions Ernie gave me and decided to go with it," Jennifer said while she took a sip of her champagne.

"I acted like I was looking for directions to Macy's, and, well, I guess the both of them hadn't talked to a woman in a long time. It was like taking candy from a baby," Jennifer said and ordered us another round.

"When I saw you, MC, I just acted like you were a friend joining me for shopping, and the rest is history. I didn't take acting lessons for nothing," Jennifer said as more cocktails arrived. We soon finished our drinks, and before long we forgot why we were there.

We were busy girlfriend chatting until Rodeo walked up. Velma and Rodeo exchanged that same look between them, and then he spoke.

"Meeting's over," he said. "Let's go." And with that, he paid for our drinks, and we followed him back up to the hotel suite.

Rodeo seated us on the sofa and chairs once again; our aunts, Jennifer, Velma and I, for what I suspected would be our debriefing. I hadn't had a chance to say anything to either Aunt Sophia or Aunt Anna to ask about what happened with Whacked Out and Wacko. Rodeo was in full-blown operative mode and took charge of speaking before the group. Charlie and Ernie were nowhere to be found.

"Aunt Sophia, please tell us about your session with the brothers, please," Rodeo asked.

"Seymour and his brother Henry were disappointed that the cards were not speaking today, but quickly got over their disappointment," Aunt Sophia said. "That's about it. Anna kept them busy eating Greek food, and Sadie kept them busy drinking shots of ouzo. Seymour and his brother Henry spent most of the time talking about their future careers in TV."

There was quiet while Rodeo waited and stared at our aunts. I guess he knew that was all he was going to get out of Aunt Sophia and Aunt Sadie, so he made one last attempt with Aunt Anna.

"That's it?" he said, looking directly at Aunt Anna.

Aunt Anna looked at him, and then Aunt Sophia looked straight at Aunt Anna with a look on her face I recognized. Aunt Anna looked back at Rodeo and said, "That's it, partner."

I knew my aunts, and I knew that was not it, but I would have to wait to talk to Aunt Sophia to see if I could pry any more from her.

Maybe the brothers had told Aunt Sophia who they worked for and that they were involved in the plot to blow up the Statue of Liberty. That could be why Aunt Sophia needed to talk to me, and Rodeo sensed this having being trained to detect this sort of stuff.

"Well ladies, you all pulled off your parts perfectly. Thank you," Rodeo said while looking at Jennifer who was smiling back with her 'it was a piece of cake' smile.

I looked over at Velma, who spoke next, "I recognized Black Snake immediately and stayed out of the lobby while Jennifer and MC kept them occupied. Once clear, they headed up to their office, and we headed back here to the bar. Now what?" Velma asked, looking directly at Rodeo.

Rodeo just looked at her and then over to Aunt Sophia, who looked like she just remembered something. "Aunt Sophia?"

"Nothing. Just that after they left, Seymour called to say he was very sorry but something had come up at work, and he didn't know if he would be able to reschedule our session before we leave New York."

"When was this?" Rodeo asked.

"Well, about a half hour ago. Aunt Anna and I had started packing along with the rest of my crew to get ready to check out and head home," Aunt Sophia said.

"Which, young man, we need to finish, or the hotel will charge us a late fee," Aunt Sophia said firmly.

Rodeo listened to what Aunt Sophia had just said and responded, "Before long, they will figure out that someone has broken into their office. That's probably why he called you, Aunt Sophia, to cancel their session."

"All of you, please finish packing and meet me back here in fifteen minutes. We are going to the rooftop where a helicopter will be waiting for us and will take you back home where, hopefully, you can begin to put all this behind you," Rodeo said. "Another helicopter ride, just what I needed. I hate flying," I muttered.

We all finished packing, met up with Rodeo and dutifully followed him, like children, out the door to the elevator.

As karma would have it, the nightmare continued because when the elevator doors opened, there were Whacked Out and Wacko.

Aunt Sophia didn't waste any time and immediately headed into the elevator, and we all followed her lead. Rodeo, like a shadow, got into the elevator as well, moving toward the back. Once we all positioned ourselves around Aunt Sophia and the brothers, she pushed the button for the lobby.

As if acting out a role in one of her public access TV shows, Aunt Sophia quickly sprang into action. "Seymour and Henry," Aunt Sophia said. "What a surprise." And then she nodded her head at us while Velma and Jennifer and smiled. "These are some friends we've met the last couple of days at the public access convention. We are all sharing a limo to the airport."

"Oh, Miss Sophia, we were trying to catch you to see if we could squeeze in that session we had to cancel at the last minute," Wacko said.

"Oh dear. Well, I don't know what to say," Aunt Sophia said.

"Snap," Whacko said. "We had something come up at the office."

"Oh really?" Aunt Sophia asked innocently, as the elevator descended.

"Yeah, there was a break-in, but nothing was taken.

Although, it looks like someone tampered with our computers," Wacko volunteered.

"Really?" Aunt Sophia said.

"That's why I don't like computers," Aunt Anna piped in. "Anyone can steal your identity."

I was listening to all this, holding my breath and feeling my eyes wanting to roll up. We were now all in the lobby. I watched as Rodeo, still a shadow, made his way to a corner and just watched.

"Well, look, we don't want to hold you up. But will you give us a call when you get back to Fish Camp?"

"Sure," Aunt Sophia said.

"We might actually be in Fish Camp in the next week or so," said Whacked Out as his brother gave him the same look I have seen Aunt Sophia give Aunt Anna many times.

Aunt Sophia just looked at Whacked Out, while Wacko gave them both a long hard look as if her third eye was attempting to find out why these two were going to be in Fish Camp.

Aunt Anna piped in, "No kidding, how come?"

Whacko answered before Whacked Out could say anything more.

"Oh, business, just business," he said.

Jennifer, for some reason, decided to get in on the action. As brilliant as she was, she was also touched with the 'I want to be a star' bug, just like my mother all those years ago. She just couldn't resist picking up that acting role she was assigned in this plot.

"Well look, boys, if you are in Fish Camp, why don't you all come down to the Full Moon Saloon and have a drink on the house?"

Their eyes just about bugged out as she said this because she pushed her girls up and center stage, right next to their noses.

I could see from the corner of my eye that Rodeo was giving her the evil eye, and Velma, who was as silent as a mouse, was giving her the 'wrap it up' look.

"We would be honored, Ma'am," Whacked Out and Wacko both said, slowly coming under the Jennifer spell.

Aunt Sophia decided to wrap up this little meeting.

"Well, Seymour and Henry, we have got to go, but I will give you a call, and we can set up a session and meet up at the Full Moon for a drink, too. They have a great spread for happy hour."

With that, Seymour and Henry gave Aunt Sophia and Jennifer a hug and scooted out the door as the living nightmare I was a part of just continued to roll on and on.

CHAPTER 24

We all stood in the lobby and waited for Rodeo as we watched those two leave and then waited some more until Rodeo was certain they were not coming back. Finally, Rodeo walked over to us and pointed back toward the elevator. This time we made it up to the roof.

Our ride home awaited us: a big black stealthy-looking helicopter equipped with guns.

Ernie was already waiting onboard. I surreptitiously looked around and saw that Charlie was nowhere to be found. We took off, and I watched as Ernie received a call and then went up front. We all heard him tell the pilot to change course. To my horror, we were swinging around, and up ahead I could see the Statue of Liberty.

"A small change of plans. We have no choice but to fly to the mission point with this bird. The Green Team still intends to take out the Statue of Liberty and has apparently accelerated the timetable on their mission. We are heading there now," Ernie said while looking at Rodeo, who looked at us and back at Ernie and silently said, "shit." Ernie spoke to us directly. "When the helicopter lands you are to stay here, and I mean *stay put*. By no means are you to leave this chopper. Do you *all* understand?" He was looking at Aunt Anna and pointing his finger at her.

We all looked at him as if he was nuts. None of us

had any intention of leaving the chopper until it landed in Fish Camp, including Aunt Anna who sat there now with her arms crossed.

We circled the Statue of Liberty and landed on Ellis Island. Ernie and Rodeo jumped out, and we could see where they were joined by a group that looked like them, Special Ops or Navy Seals, just your standard Homeland Security.

As we sat there for what seemed like hours, fog drifted in from the sea and covered us like a shield. The pilot, up front, remained alert and poised like a sentry.

I looked over at Jennifer, who was now catching up on her beauty sleep. She had taken a small travel pillow out of her bag and had placed cucumbers over her eyes.

The rest of us were surprisingly quiet. Velma had her eyes closed, but I suspected she wasn't asleep because she had that look on her face she usually reserved for Rodeo. Aunt Anna, like Jennifer, was sleeping and now she was snoring. I watched in amazement as Velma's Aunt Sadie bided the time either texting or playing games on her cell.

Aunt Sophia pretty much stared straight ahead at the water, out a window across from where we both sat as if she could see the ship that had brought her parents, my grandparents, from Greece to Ellis Island.

I leaned over to her now and said, "What did you want to talk to me about?"

She thought for a moment and said, still staring out the window, "Oh, it was something that had to do with what Seymour said back at the hotel."

I waited for her to tell me while she was still staring ahead deep in thought.

"What?" I finally said.

"Nothing," she said. Fine, I thought, while I took a deep breath.

"Just that he was with the government, just like you were," Aunt Sophia said.

"Oh," I said. Well, that just confirmed in my mind that those two did work for Walther Roosevelt.

"They're both here to practice a military exercise," she said while she nodded in the direction of the Statue of Liberty, which was now shrouded in fog.

"What do you mean?"

"A military exercise, but it's only practice according to Seymour, you know like a dress rehearsal for a play.

"They were supposed to act like they were after terrorists who were going to blow up the Statue of Liberty. I suspect Ernie and Rodeo have found this out while they were out there chasing them around Ellis Island."

"Aunt Sophia," I heard my voice an octave higher now. "Why didn't you say anything when we were having our meeting with Rodeo?"

"Because, as I told Rodeo on day one, it's part of my confidentiality agreement with my clients as a reader of the cards. What goes on during the reading stays in the reading. I can't reveal it until it reveals itself. You know that," she said while she looked at me and nodded her head.

They're smart enough, those two, and I knew they would find out for themselves before long."

"Okay," I said. "So why are you telling me this now?"

She just looked straight ahead and nodded her head toward the window. "That's why."

As I looked out the window, I saw shadows coming into view through the fog. The next thing I knew, Whacked Out and Wacko climbed in, and the conversation picked up right where we left it in the lobby of the Waldorf Astoria lobby.

Velma opened her eyes, looked at me, but didn't move since we were both numb. Our aunts seemed to be right at home with this scenario. Jennifer was now snoring.

Wacko looked at us, and then Whacked Out said, "Aunt Sophia, what are you doing here?"

"Hello Henry," Aunt Sophia said. "I think I told you that my niece, MC, also worked for the government," she said as she nodded her head toward me.

"I see," Wacko said as he and his brother Whacked Out settled in, joined the group. The two brothers were not one to think down in the weeds. They were happy to follow orders.

In another minute both Rodeo and Ernie boarded, followed by Charlie. Once we were all on board, Charlie, who was now sitting on the other side of me, leaned over and whispered in my ear, "Dominic didn't show."

I heard myself say as I looked at him, "Really?"

A minute passed while we all stared out the window as the helicopter took off, and we flew right over the Statue of Liberty.

"She looks fine," Aunt Sophia whispered in my ear. "See the crown is all intact as well as the rest of her. Her light shines brightly through the fog, just as it did those many years ago when your grandparents arrived at Ellis Island."

I watched Lady Liberty as we flew further away. She was safe for now. Her beam of light shone brightly for all it stood for and then disappeared in the dark.

We watched as the chopper landed on top of Trump Tower. I thought, 'What next? Will Trump meet us when we land?' Instead, it was more Homeland Security types.

"Ok, you will stay with the Seals, and they will escort you all back to the Astoria, where you'll wait until you hear from me," Rodeo said to Velma and me as we all made our way out of the chopper. He then added, looking straight at Velma, "We are heading out to track down the Green Team leader, Black Snake. He got away with Dirt Devil. We think they are heading out of the city by subway."

Velma just stared at him and looked into his eyes, and before I knew it, she reached up and gave Rodeo a kiss and a long embrace and said, "Be careful."

He looked deep into her eyes and then was gone. Velma and I watched as the Wacko brothers followed Rodeo, and then met up with Ernie. In a second, they were gone, like shadows at high noon. I looked up just as the helicopter lifted off Trump pad, and there was Charlie, on the pad, looking at me. He waved good-bye, and before long, he disappeared into the clouds.

CHAPTER 25

We made our way back to the hotel with our Navy Seal escort, who had fallen deeply under the Jennifer spell and made sure we landed safe and sound back at the Waldorf.

We were back in the same hotel suite, and I collapsed into a large, cushy armchair. It had been calling my name. Just as I was closing my eyes, ready to drift off, I heard a loud voice. It was Aunt Sadie.

"Listen up. I just got a call and my niece Cassie's here. Come on, we're going after the bad guys."

"What are you talking about?"

"Cassie is downstairs double parked in Birdie, her Bluebird RV."

I looked at Aunt Sophia and Aunt Anna, who just stared back with the old 'Greek woman stare down' look. I then glanced at Jennifer and Velma, who both had blank expressions on their faces, although I thought for a second Jennifer had the 'I'm sorry' look on her face. The one I had recognized after my meeting with her when she had told me that Aunt Sophia was her psychic.

"Aunt Sophia," I said.

Aunt Sophia stood up and took center stage, just like Ernie had a little while earlier. She now looked like she was in full operative mode.

"Your mother came to Aunt Sadie in a dream and told her that Cassie needed to hightail it to New York City in Birdie."

"Oh?" I remarked. "Go on." The nightmare was back on and taking on a distinctly surreal feeling as if I was looking at a Dali painting and trying to make out the inner meaning.

"Yes," Aunt Sophia said. "In the dream, we were all at the St. James where, you know, the musical, *Grand Ole Opry*, is now playing."

"All." I was afraid to ask who "all" meant. Probably the rest of the crew including Molly and Harold, who, I thought, had returned home safely.

"So, Aunt Sadie had a dream where Mom directed her to tell Cassie to get to New York City in her RV, and we were all going over to the St. James in that comfy, large vehicle."

Aunt Sophia came over, sat next to me and took my hands in hers.

"MC, dreams are not laid out like a movie in a straight line, much like life," she said looking directly into my eyes. "I looked at the cards and put this all together. Your mother was sending us a message. And ... let's just say, to get the rest of the story we need to make our way over to the St. James. It's in the cards, too, and we have no choice but to follow it through to the end. It will happen, one way or another, whether we like it or not. So, we might as well get it over with, once and for all."

I sat there for a minute and realized that I had no control over the situation. Despite being the "control queen," it was out of control and definitely out of my hands.

"OK," I said. "Let's get this over with. How do you plan to get by the two trained Seals stationed right outside the door?"

"Jennifer?" Aunt Sophia said as we looked in her direction.

Of course, I should have known, the Jennifer spell. And, with that, she unbuttoned the top two buttons of her blouse, pushed up her girls and went to work. While Jennifer had the highly trained Seals under her spell, Velma seemed to take over and led us through the suite and out the other door.

I looked down the hall and could see that Jennifer had the Seals looking the other way. They were mesmerized by Jennifer, who was leaning forward to give them both a good look at the girls, who were up front and center. We all made our way to the elevator and out the lobby of the grand hotel where Cassie really was double parked and waiting out front. We all piled into the RV, and I gave Cassie 'The Look.' She just smiled back with the same smile I usually got from Velma. The 'don't ask' smile.

Velma jumped in next to Cassie, and we made our way around the block. When we returned, Jennifer was waiting for us with her girls back under wraps.

She hopped in, and before I knew it, we were all in the Bluebird and heading over to the St. James where the musical, *Grand Ole Opry*, was playing.

I looked around, and yes, there were Molly and Harold, just as I had suspected. I'm not sure why, but my little voice told me to follow along and go with the flow. Here we were, my two aunts, Velma, Cassie and their Aunt Sadie, Harold and Molly and me, driving down the center of Broadway in an RV. Someone was missing. I looked around, and out of the corner of my eye, to my consternation, there was Izzy perched up high, on one of the overhead bins.

Cassie caught my look and said, "You didn't think we'd leave him home alone in your office, did you?"

At this point, I was petrified, especially with Cassie driving the big old RV, cabbie horns honking all around us. At that moment, I decided that the job opening at the recreation center was where I was headed if we all survived this. I'm sure, with training, I can learn how to teach a Zumba class. Please, Saint Anthony, I prayed silently, make this nightmare over soon, and a lot of cash donations will come your way.

After Cassie somehow managed to park Birdie the RV in the back of the theater, we entered through the side entrance. Molly knew the way having danced on most of the boards on Broadway.

As we entered the theater, I could see two men on the stage. They didn't look like actors, and Velma let out a sigh. She recognized them. There stood Black Snake and Dirt Devil, and it felt as if they were waiting for us.

"Well, well, well, what do we have here?" They pointed their two M-16s at us and told us to have a seat in the front row. Nice seats.

As we sat there, all lined up as if we were waiting for the matinee performance, Aunt Anna got up and started hollering at them in Greek. Not only was she hollering, but she also began to spit at them, and the next thing I knew, she had managed to make her way on stage hollering and now was in close spitting range.

Black Snake and Dirt Devil looked at her in a daze for a minute, taken back a little by Aunt Anna's performance, and then Black Snake raised the M16 as if to shoot her.

Dirt Devil now hollered at Black Snake and said, "Wait a minute. You can't shoot the old woman."

"Why not?" said Black Snake.

"Why not?" Dirt Devil said. "You are asking me why not? Because it would be bad luck. She threatened to put a hex on us if we killed anyone in their group."

"You don't believe in that nonsense, do you?" Black Snake snarled at Dirt Devil. "What are you, hanging out in looney land like those two Whacko brothers?"

"Yes, I do. She has the evil eye," Dirt Devil said, and then the fight began. Aunt Anna kept up her tirade, and then Aunt Sophia and Aunt Sadie stood up and started in like they were her backup singers, Aunt Sophia spitting and hollering in Greek, and Aunt Sadie with some serious jive trash.

We were all sitting there mesmerized when the next thing I heard was Velma saying, "Come on, we got to do something."

Velma got up, and Cassie and Jennifer followed her like zombies up onto the other side of the stage. I found myself teleported right behind them. Just about the time we reached the stage, Aunt Anna had thrown her big black purse at Black Snake. It hit Dirt Devil instead, but it was a bull's eye.

What happened next could not have been choreographed better for a Broadway show. We were all rolling, all over the stage, and the M-16's were hopping back and forth as if a military drill was taking place. The purse had managed to throw Dirt Devil off balance. You would have thought that purse was a bullet, but then we all froze. Black Snake had Aunt Anna pinned, and he had a knife pressing into her neck.

"The fun and games are over. All of you, down on the floor, now," Black Snake said. "You too, Dirt Devil. You can join them since you're so afraid of these old women. Drop your weapon and push it over this way."

We all got down on the floor including Dirt Devil, who followed instructions. Once down, all we could do was watch as Black Snake tightened his hold on Aunt Anna.

I was staring hard at Aunt Anna trying to tell her not to make a move, but she started squirming, and I saw it as if I had been watching a play right on the stage. The nasty, ink-colored eyes of Black Snake told me he was going to take out Aunt Anna before our eyes.

I couldn't let that happen. This time, I was not going to turn off the voice in my head; I was going to listen. I stood up on stage, and thanks to some plyometric jump training I learned at a boot camp class, I quickly leaped at him with no plan other than to distract him.

Before I knew it, Dirt Devil jumped up and pushed Black Snake away from Aunt Anna, but unfortunately, right at me. He knocked me down, and I knew I was dead because, as he raised his arm to throw the knife at me, I could see, standing next to him, a vision of my mother in her power suit, black pumps, and black church pocketbook. The one that was as big as a suitcase.

Great, I thought, she was coming for me, and, even scarier, she looked mad.

What happened next, I will remember for the rest of

my life and wonder if it was pure fear, or if it really happened. For some reason, Black Snake stopped and looked over in her direction, as if he was directly staring at my mother.

As I looked, I saw her spit in his eye and slap him on the head with her black pocketbook. Then Rodeo came out of nowhere and tackled Black Snake. After some slick martial arts maneuvers, Black Snake was out cold.

Ernie and the other Special Ops soldiers came in and cuffed Dirt Devil and Black Snake and carted them both off stage right.

As they were taking Dirt Devil away, Ernie came up to him and said it would not be forgotten what he did today. Dirt Devil nodded, and as he was walking across the stage, took a bow toward Aunt Anna who blew him a kiss.

I woke up from this dream to see Aunt Sophia standing over me as she gently shook me.

She was leaning down and saying, "Are you all right?"

I realized that I must have fallen asleep on the oversized chair in the hotel suite.

"Yes," I said. I realized I was coming out of what must have been a dream, but it was one of those very realistic dreams we all have from time to time. The 'thank goodness it was just a dream and not the real thing' feeling swept over me.

"I was dreaming. It was a dream, but one of those dreams that felt as if I was in the dream. I think you know what I mean," I said to Aunt Sophia, while she stared at me as I shook off the dream.

Aunt Sophia continued to stare at me and then said, "You were in a place called Dreamland. It's between the visible and invisible world. Tell me about the dream, MC."

Since it was fresh in my mind, I told Aunt Sophia all about the dream or what I thought was a dream.

When I finished, Aunt Sophia said, "MC, get on your cell and call Ernie."

Without any protest, I did exactly as my Aunt Sophia directed. Instinctively, I knew what she thought because, weirdly, so did I. When I heard Ernie's voice, I handed her my cell.

"Ernie, this is Sophia, you need to hightail it over to the theater where the *Grand Ole Opry* is playing. You'll find what you are looking for there."

She handed me back my cell.

"Got it," I heard Ernie say, and then he hung up, no questions asked.

I looked at Aunt Sophia, and she looked back at me. She came over and gave me a hug and said, "You know that was more than a dream, MC?"

"Yes," I said. "I do now, Aunt Sophia."

She continued to stare at me and then said, "Good, let's get ready to head home."

Later I heard from Ernie. They found the other two at the theater just like my dream.

Ernie said they were able to take them down, and Black Snake kept mumbling something about a vision of a large woman in black pumps, with a big black purse, who kept spitting in his face. "It was very odd," Ernie said. "But we got them."

We made it back to Fish Camp later that night with our military escort. For the first time in a long time, I slept with no dreams and woke only once when the light flickered on.

*Well, Mom, you finally made it to Broadway, and now your dream to become a star finally came true. I love you, too.* I closed my eyes and slept for what seemed like an eternity.

CHAPTER 26

What happened next seemed like a sequel to the movie that started a few weeks ago when Babbs and Jennifer had first shown up in my office. It was all over the evening and cable news and the newspapers that a major terrorist plot to blow up the Statue of Liberty had been thwarted by an elite group of Navy Seals.

We were all told by Ernie to keep a lid on it, and we were all more than happy to oblige and put this whole ordeal in our rearview mirror. Ernie and Rodeo were not mentioned. I guess they were more valuable as shadows.

Walther Roosevelt, on the other hand, was now a household name. As the head of the government's war on terror program, he became the anointed spokesperson and didn't pass up any opportunity to take credit for this major takedown of terrorists.

The plot to blow up the Statue of Liberty was blamed on some unknown new crop of terrorists. When questioned by the press, Walther responded that they were being pursued, but details were not available due to national security.

Velma and I rolled our eyes every time someone mentioned Walther's name, which lately, not to our surprise, was now cited as a rising star in the world of politics.

"This is no different than being back at the IRS, working in a vacuum," I said to Velma as we read the latest news. "This was a well-played act orchestrated by Walther Roosevelt and his terrorists played by the Green Team just to pump up his stock in the public eye."

Right now, all Velma and I knew was that the Green Team had disappeared along with their leader, Black Snake. Who knows where they are? Maybe part of some witness protection plan for freelance, covert operators. Maybe Walther arranged for their jobs to be axed and a nice buyout, just like he did for Velma and me.

Velma did share with me what I assumed was now pillow talk, that Rodeo had told her not to worry about Black Snake. He was gone and would probably never be seen again.

"Rodeo and Ernie uncovered and traced information about cash that had been delivered to Black Snake. It appeared to be an off the books cash hoard, to be used for the alleged terrorist attack on the Statue of Liberty," she shared. "That's interesting. They might want to hang onto that information for future in case they need it," I said.

As for Charlie, the story that was floated was Charlie had gone fishing and at the last minute changed his plans and went to Costa Rica. While fishing, he had imbibed a little too much rum and fallen overboard. He was in a coma in a hospital in Costa Rica. When he woke up, they released him, and he returned home. This only added further luster to his bad boy, but good guy, image.

After a while, the gossip died down, and life returned to the certain calmness, it had been before. End of story, or at least that's all I was going to get out of Velma, and I was surprised I even got that much. Ernie had probably given her the okay to release the information to me so that I would stop bugging him every time I saw him at the Hotel Florida. The drinks on the house were beginning to add up.

So, all was back to normal except for the elephant in the room named Dominic. In the back of all our minds, we knew it was just a matter of time before Dominic made his move to take over the grocery business and turn it into a laundromat. But Ernie would also not rest until Dominic was taken out for the murder of his comrade, Harry West.

One morning when I had just finished my Cuban coffee, I looked up to see Velma standing in my office door and next to her was the elephant. It proceeded to walk into my office and sit down in the same chair as Queen Babbs from what now seemed to be some previous lifetime.

Dominic sat there, cool as a cucumber with his legs crossed and just stared at me. He then lifted his arms and snapped his fingers and said, "Velma, you may as well come in and have a seat. Your boss here may need your assistance." The nightmare was back.

Velma sat down next to him. We watched as he got up, walked over and looked out the window.

"Ah, *Pirate Life*, she's looking well. I won her in a poker game a few years back," Dominic said staring out the window at the yacht. He came back and stood next to the side of my desk and got right down to business.

"I need my cash back. I expect you, MC, with all your skills can locate it. I will give you and your assistant Velma here 24 hours to retrieve it and bring it back to this office. I will meet you both here tomorrow night. If it's not here then … well MC, you and your feisty friend Velma will be taking a little cruise with me on *Pirate Life*. You don't want that to happen, would you ladies?"

He was now leaning on the side of my desk and had come close to both of us by placing both his hands on the edge, allowing him to rock in really close and whisper, "No word of this to your two friends, Ernie or Rodeo, or my Aunt Babbs, or Charlie. You are to keep them all out of this. Do you both understand?" he said, as he rocked back to standing.

"This applies to the both of you." Then he leaned over and pounded his fist on the center of my desk to make sure we got his point. While we were both recovering from a little jump reflex to his pounding on my desk, he added the deal maker, "For the sake of your dear aunts, that cash better be sitting right here on this desk in 24 hours."

To make sure we knew where the cash should be sitting he pounded on the desk one more time. We watched him now as he walked over to the window and looked out at *Pirate Life* as if he could see his future. He turned, and we watched the elephant stomp out of our office. We sat there for a few minutes, unable to move. I looked over at Velma who rose quietly and went up front. I could hear her talking to someone on the phone.

She came back to my desk and said, "Let's go."

"Where are we going?"

"I just called Rodeo, and we are going to meet Rodeo and Ernie and Charlie at the Hotel Florida."

I got up from my desk, walked over and looked out at *Pirate Life*. Velma came over and stood next to me. "Let's do it," I said, and out the door we went.

CHAPTER 27

As soon as we sat down in the car, my cell rang. When I answered, it was Ernie. "Meet us at my houseboat," was all he said and hung up. I told Velma to drive to Ernie's houseboat, and when we arrived we were greeted by Ernie, who took us to the main salon where we saw Rodeo and Charlie, and not to my surprise, Jennifer was sitting with a briefcase. I had no doubt now that the briefcase was not empty since it was fully expanded. Ernie was back in full operative mode.

"MC, we knew Dominic would contact you before too long," Ernie said.

Velma and Jennifer were quiet, for a change, but I piped up and asked the 'no question is ever too stupid' question, "How did you know that?"

Ernie filled us in. "The Green Team, if you recall, worked for the feds as freelance operatives hired by Mr. Walther Roosevelt, who is presently sitting pretty and is being mentioned by all the talking heads as our next vice president. What you may not have known is that, in the past, the four of them also worked for a good friend of Walther's, a guy by the name of Jack Spoto. Mr. Spoto is a major defense contractor located in Cocoa Beach.

"Let's just say that Rodeo and I set up a meeting with Mr. Spoto at his favorite watering hole in Cocoa

Beach and told him that it was his patriotic duty to share with us whatever information he had regarding the terrorist plot to take down the Statue of Liberty."

"Really," I said.

Ernie continued. "Well, while we talked, we pointed out to him something we suspected after Rodeo's visit to the Green Team's office in New York, that we were pretty sure the cash used to engage the Green Team was cash skimmed from his super PAC. We also added that his good friend, Walther Roosevelt, would probably drop him like a hot potato if all this was mysteriously leaked to the media.

"In the end, it went well for the both of them. Mr. Roosevelt is sitting pretty, and so is Jack. His business is on the upswing with the renewed interest by our country on the ever-present danger of terrorist attacks. Let's just say we have Jack in our pocket if we ever need him," Ernie said. And more than likely the evidence to back it up I thought. "Rodeo and I are also back working for Homeland and have been watching our friend, Dominic, who we now have confirmed is connected with some real terrorists," Ernie said.

"We figured that, before long, Dominic would have a meeting coming up, not unlike what Boris was facing a few weeks ago when he needed those cookbooks. Dominic needs all the cash back. He was supposed to be laundering it through the grocery business," Ernie was on a roll I thought.

"His prospective clients have lost patience with him while he stalled them with his waiting for his father's health to take a nose dive. The word is that they have told Dominic he has three days to return the cash to them because they have decided to go elsewhere to clean their money."

"Really," I said.

"Dominic has always been a high roller. While sitting on the cash he should have been laundering, he has been gambling. He's spent and lost a lot of money and is scrambling now to get back to square one. If he can get his hands on it, he's probably going to turn over the cash to this group to stall them while he takes off to somewhere like Costa Rica for a while," Ernie said.

"We figured that he would use you, MC, to get the cash back for him. Now, we are going to take him down along with some real terrorists."

I felt a shudder go down my spine. Someone was walking on my grave.

"What's the plan?" I heard myself and Velma saying at the same time.

"You will meet Dominic tomorrow night, as planned, in your office. You will have the cash. When he walks in, we'll take over. Simple." Nothing was simple, and somehow, I knew it, but again I was along for the ride.

"Okay," I said. "But how are you going to take

down the terrorists?"

"You will give Dominic the cash. We have word that he has contacted the terrorists and will meet them right after he picks up the cash from you to turn it over to them."

"Wait a minute. Won't he just shoot Velma and me?"

"He probably would if we weren't going to show up along with a team from the FBI. They will offer him a deal, and he will take it being the little chicken of the sea he is, and then he will lead us to the terrorists."

"Now wait just a minute. You mean he's going to get witness protection?" Charlie was talking now.

"Charlie, I don't like this any more than you, but it's for the greater good," Ernie said.

Charlie just looked at him, and I could tell he wasn't buying into this scenario. He was angry and said, "I got it. Just like Jack, who is using that super PAC like a personal petty cash fund for his buddy Walther, will get a pass. You are just following orders, I get that, but I don't have to like it. That little snake will find his way back home. And what about Harry West? What about what really is going on here? Those two are making a mockery of 9/11. They could care less about the fact that we have lost sight of that day and all who lost their lives on that day," Charlie said."

Ernie stood his ground, but his mind was wobbling.

"We need Dominic. He can get us to the terrorists," he said.

Charlie thought about that and let it simmer right there for the moment. He still wasn't happy, judging from the look on his face.

"The FBI is in the driver's seat now," Ernie continued. Then he turned to us and said, "MC and Velma, you will both have to wear a wire. Are you up to it?" Now it was Rodeo's turn.

"Velma? Why does Velma have to wear a wire?"

"Rodeo," Velma said, and that was all Velma had to say.

They exchanged a look, and I knew they would talk later.

I heard my little voice talking now.

"I don't like it," I said. "I just don't like the whole setup. Dominic will be given a pass by the feds, and believe me, he will wiggle his way back. And, even if he doesn't, we will all have to watch our backs until we're old and gray. We have to put him away for good. And Charlie is right. I'm not going to stand by and watch Walther Roosevelt make a mockery of 9/11, primarily since he saw fit to ax our jobs. No deal."

Ernie walked over to the bar and poured himself a shot of tequila and then said, "What do you have in mind?"

He passed the bottle around, and we all took a drink

straight from the bottle, like the pirates we were. Charlie spoke next. It was going to take someone who could think like a scoundrel to take down Dominic. "MC, you still have Boris as your best bud, right?" Charlie asked.

"Yes," I said. "I do."

"We are going let Boris take Dominic down. He is the only one with the manpower and the heart. Once he knows terrorists are operating in his backyard, well, 'Katy bar the door.'"

We all thought about this for a moment, and Charlie was right about Boris.

"No wires. No FBI. Ernie, you will have to stall them. MC and Velma, you will sit tight there in your office.

"He will have men watching so it will look like you both are here as planned to meet with him tomorrow night to deliver the cash. Can you do it?"

"Yes," we both said in unison, I am sure we were both thinking of the safety of our aunts.

I heard Velma now. "I'm in on this, and I'll be right there with MC."

Rodeo just rolled his eyes and said, "Not without me in the shadows."

It was now Ernie's choice.

"Well, I never wanted to go back to work anyway.

OK, I'm in," said Ernie."

Jennifer had been sitting there all this time as quiet as a mouse.

She spoke next.

"What is my part? I have an interest in this because, ever since he arrived in town, Dominic has been breathing down my neck, and I need to shake him loose. I don't need another mafia husband. Nor do I need Joe and Dominic fighting over me. Joe is aware of Dominic and said as much one night at the Full Moon. And I'd hate to lose Joe."

Charlie looked at Jennifer, and I could see his mind working as if he had thought this all the way through, instantly, as only a pirate with a genius IQ was capable of doing.

"Jennifer, you, my dear, are going to cast your magic spell on Dominic and get him to meet you at the Full Moon Saloon. Arrange it for early afternoon, and tell him you would like to invite him for a drink. We will let Boris take over from that point. Instead of witness protection, Boris can offer him life or death for the terrorists and then deliver Dominic to the sheriff for the murder of Harry West," Charlie said.

"MC, you and Velma will be waiting back at your office until you hear that the coast is clear. If all goes as planned, Dominic won't be able to resist showing up at the Full Moon Saloon," Charlie said. At that point Ernie, you and Rodeo can take over and do your part."

We all broke for the night and made our way home.

It all sounded like a good plan, but something was telling me that the black cloud was still hanging over my head. On my way back to my condo, I was sure I saw Dominic's Mercedes following me, but then, it could have been my imagination. I would just be glad when I woke from this nightmare. As I walked into my condo, I pinched myself, and it felt like a needle prick. Snap. This time I was awake, and it wasn't a dream.

CHAPTER 28

When I got to my office the following morning, I found myself right back in the hot seat, along with Velma, who was sitting right across from my desk in full Velma mode. The plan that Charlie had laid out yesterday on the houseboat was simple. Jennifer was to give Dominic a call and invite him for a drink at the Full Moon Saloon. He would show up because he was no different than Ernie or any other man who had fallen under her spell: brain dead. Once he showed, Joe would pick a fight with him, and then Boris and his crew would jump into the barroom brawl, and when it was over Dominic, would be gone from our lives for good.

Ernie, however, must have thought it over last night and made other plans as to how this was going to go down today. Number one, he was going to make sure that they got the terrorists. When I walked through the door, Velma told me that Ernie had made a call to his new best bud, Jack Spoto, to get word to his bud, Walther Roosevelt, to get ready to do his job and take down some real terrorists, or he would make sure they were both the lead story on that night's evening news. So, what had been a clean and simple plan to get rid of Dominic had become complicated because Walther called in his Green Team, and they were now in my office in full operative mode.

Dirt Devil was at the window looking out at *Pirate*

*Life*. He explained to both Velma and me that they would be going after the terrorists, once they got the word from Ernie that Boris had taken care of Dominic. Boris would get the location of the meeting out of Dominic and let Ernie know where he could find the terrorists. Ernie was going to personally deliver a message to the leader of the terrorists. He would let him know that Dominic wasn't going to make their meeting, and they would find what was left of their cash, which Dominic had been using for gambling debts, at MC's office. And if they hurried, they could catch Dominic, who was on his way to pick it up and then had plans to disappear. As soon as they got the word from Ernie that the terrorists were heading to my office, the Green Team would descend and take care of business.

That was all Dirt Devil said to us. It was clear to Velma and me that he was now in charge of the Green Team. Wacked Out walked over to us and whispered, "Don't worry. We will make sure nothing happens to you or your dear aunts."

Velma looked up at him and said, "You better make sure nothing happens to our aunts, you numbskull. Or I will personally see to it that you and your brother over there are pushing up daisies in the boneyard."

He just looked at Velma, then at me and retreated to the other side of the office with his brother, Wacko. Velma, to my consternation, was not finished.

"So, what is it with you three stiffs working both sides of the street?"

It was Dirt Devil's turn now. He walked over and stood next to my desk, right where Dominic had stood yesterday.

"We are not idealists. I think you know them as politicians. This is our profession, and we offer our services to the highest bidder. It's a business, and we do what we do very well."

Velma just looked at him for a moment, gave him the evil eye, closed her eyes, and went back into waiting mode. I just looked at Dirt Devil, who made his way back to the window and continued to stare out at *Pirate Life*. We didn't have to wait long because his cell rang, and while he answered, we all watched him.

He closed his cell and announced, "It's done. Dominic is no longer your problem. Boris and his men have done their job. Your friend Jennifer is safe."

"Good," Velma said next. "Now, can we get out of here and let you three do your job?"

"No, I'm afraid not. We have word that the terrorists have been spotted en route to this location and will be here shortly. We don't want to tip them off. It's best for you two to stay put in this office. You will be safe. Let's go," he said to the Wacko brothers, and all three went out the front door.

Velma got up and looked out the window at *Pirate Life*.

"I don't think we should stay here. I have a bad

feeling about this."

"Velma, please sit down and let them do their job. I'm pretty sure that the area is surrounded by operatives, Seals, and who knows what else. I think I spotted a drone out that window a few minutes ago."

"Yeah, well, I'm not sitting here."

"Okay then, where are you going?"

Out there, she pointed with her head. I got up and looked out the window at *Pirate Life*.

"Are you saying we are going to stow away on *Pirate Life*?"

"Yes, just until this whole thing blows over. I feel like a sitting duck here in this office."

I thought about what she had said, and she had a point. I caved in, and the next thing I knew we had pried open the back window. "You go first," Velma said. So, I hopped out the window and jumped to the dock. I turned around to see Velma coming next with Izzy.

We made our way over to *Pirate Life* and were now sitting in the back of the yacht as if we were waiting for cocktails. From where we sat it was dark, but we could see the office, which was quiet. We felt alone, but we both knew there was an army out there in the shadows. This went on for several hours, and we both dozed off until we heard a noise. It was Izzy, and he was snarling at what must have been Dominic's ghost, who was boarding with a couple of his men.

"Well, well, well, what do we have here, a couple of stowaways and a rat?" Izzy snarled and then moved closer to Velma.

As he boarded, I could see he was carrying the briefcase, which he tapped while he said to us, "Your friend Boris almost had me, but I managed to get away thanks to your friend Joe, who wasn't going to let anything happen to Jennifer."

"Let's just say I traded Jennifer for the briefcase. Charlie was very helpful in delivering it to me. Don't worry they're all back at the bar licking their wounds, but since you two are here, you may not be joining them anytime soon. Let's go," he hollered. "Get her out in the gulf where we can dump these two and that rat." Then he leaned a little closer to Velma. "Don't worry, with all that Danish you've been eating, you should sink with no problem."

He went down below with the briefcase. We both sat there with one of his men, who no doubt would be happy to shoot us if we moved. I looked over at Velma who appeared surprisingly calm.

Unfortunately, I didn't expect to see my mother since I knew she had never learned to swim. I sat there while we headed through the canals down the Intracoastal Waterway, and before long we were anchored in the Atlantic. I couldn't believe it was all coming down to this, a watery grave.

I sat there with my eyes closed saying what I feared were my last prayers to Saint Anthony and anyone else up there who could hear me. I had sunk into a meditative state and was having a one-on-one with my mother and my grandmother. In this state of mind, I could see them. The two of them were silent, which was very odd. They just seemed to be staring at me. Then the fight began between those two in my mind's eye. Really!

I opened my eyes, let out a big sigh and looked over at Velma. She was staring at me about the same way my mother and grandmother had been staring at me in my altered state of mind. Scary. I watched her as she turned her head. I followed her gaze out to sea as she continued to stare out into the black night.

I looked out, and all I could see was darkness and the cold black sea below the darkness. The trance was broken as Dominic appeared on the deck as if to see us off. He walked over to us, hovered and stared at the both of us. I could not see his eyes in the dark, but I felt their stare, and it felt black and evil.

Dominic turned and walked to the front of the boat. He was busy now talking to his henchmen. They had long anchor chains and were attempting to attach them to two large anchors. One anchor for me and one anchor for Velma to carry us both swiftly to our final resting place, Davy Jones Locker.

As they were about to wrap up attaching the chains to the anchors, Dominic looked at us and then signaled the man who was watching us to the front of the boat to help.

"Say your prayers, ladies," he shouted to us and then turned his attention to his men and the task at hand at the front of the boat.

Although I knew Velma was right next to me, I suddenly felt truly alone. I felt my breathing slow, mustering up final breaths for what was soon to happen. As I stared at the anchor and chains at the front of the boat waiting to drag Velma and me to our graves, my eyes instinctively moved to the side of the boat.

Out of the shadows and a sea fog, which would serve as our shroud, I thought I was looking at an apparition. Pirates from long ago were now coming for us. Ironically, my life was coming to an end on *Pirate Life*. My fear was being replaced with shock, the body's natural anesthesia.

As I stared into the black night, I felt my eyes focus on three apparitions rising from the dark water. As I watched, they seemed to float up from the sea, out of the fog and were now slowly gliding toward Velma and me.

I came out of my state of shock when I heard Velma take a deep breath and say, "Thank you, Lord."

As if I was waking up from anesthesia, I was looking at Rodeo and two Navy Seals, who I recognized from New York, and they never looked better.

Rodeo bent down close to Velma and said, "You and MC get down below. NOW." So, we did, quicker than a New York minute. As we scampered below, I almost tripped as Izzy appeared and shot passed us.

We quickly found a cabin, shut the door, and huddled together, not speaking a word for what appeared to be another lifetime. Above us, we could hear shots and what sounded like helicopters and … then there was silence. After a few moments, I heard footsteps approaching our cabin, I closed my eyes and crouched down as the cabin door opened. "It's over, ladies," Rodeo said as he walked into the cabin and gave Velma a quick embrace. He then looked at me and frowned.

"I thought you two had strict orders to stay in your office," he said. He looked at us and shook his head. He continued, "MC, for a minute I thought I was going to regret not getting you out on the range. It looks like you won't need that weapons training after all," he said with a big sigh, as he looked at Velma with the look he reserved only for her. "Thank God," he said. "Dominic and his men are all dead," Rodeo said, back in full operative mode as he turned to head back up on deck.

We sat there, and soon we heard the engines rev up and the boat moved. I looked over at Velma, who had her eyes closed. I did the same and fell asleep as *Pirate Life* made its way back home. I awoke as I felt the boat docking. For a second I thought I remembered a dream. It was my mother, and she was shaking her finger at me, but for once she wasn't talking.

Back in my office, I looked out the window and could see the first rays of dawn. *Pirate Life* was gone. I was sitting at my desk, and Velma was sitting across from me. Izzy was snoring on his perch.

The office was full of Navy Seals, Homeland Security, and who knew what else. Ernie and Rodeo were there and back in full operative mode. The Green Team was nowhere to be seen. Rodeo walked over to us and handed us two steaming cups of Cuban coffee. He leaned down and whispered to us that the Green Team had taken care of the terrorists.

In the days that followed, Walther was again all over the news, this time taking real credit for the takedown of the terrorists, who he reported was the group behind the plans to blow up the Statue of Liberty. Walther was in his element. The talking heads were referring to him as someone to watch as a future potential presidential candidate.

The local news reported that Dominic had been killed when the local sheriff went after him as he tried escaping on his yacht, *Pirate Life*. The story said that the sheriff had been about to arrest him for the murder of local private eye, Harry West, who had been hired by Queen Babbs because she suspected he was skimming cash from the grocery business. Harry West found out that Dominic had plans to launder mob money through the family grocery business, and that's why he killed Harry West.

The news also reported that Sal was back from the dead, and Queen Babbs and her husband Charlie had taken off for an extended second honeymoon.

A few more weeks went by, and from time to time I would ask Velma about the elephant still sitting in my office. What happened to the briefcase of cash Dominic had brought on board *Pirate Life*? I knew she knew because no doubt she got it out of Rodeo. She just looked at me and gave me her 'if I told you I'd have to shoot you' look. So, I guess things were back to normal.

One quiet afternoon I left the office early and decided to go over to the Hotel Florida to have a brew on my way home. Ernie came over, and by the look on my face, he could tell I was thinking about all that had happened in the last couple of months. He placed a beer in front of me and said, "The beer is on the house." I was happy with that, but in the back of my mind my accounting synapses were not happy and were firing away.

Rodeo showed up and flashed his beautiful smile. Funny how, more and more as Velma's daughters grew older, their smiles matched the one Rodeo flashed.

I stayed for one more brew, said my good-byes and headed out to my car to make my way home.

I got in my car and put all the windows down, feeling the breeze. I just sat there for the longest time thinking about everything that had happened since that day when Babbs and Jennifer had walked into my office. Just when I decided to pull out, I heard a tap on the passenger side of my car, and the next thing I knew Rodeo was sitting next to me in my car.

"What I'm about to tell you I will deny, but I am telling you because I know you, and you won't let it alone, so pay attention," he said as his dark eyes looked into mine.

"That briefcase of cash you have been asking Velma about because you just can't get your mind off of it because of your need to always make sure the books are balanced. Well, it's sitting in a safe deposit box for now, right next to the safe deposit box your cash is in, which I assume will put you in a higher tax bracket next year when you file your tax returns."

"It is?" I said. "Well, whose name is on that safe deposit box?"

Rodeo looked straight at me and said, "Uncle Sam."

"Uncle Sam?"

"That's right. Orders came from Walther Roosevelt to place the cash in a safe deposit box. End of story. So, go home and leave it alone."

"That's it? Walther ordered the cash to be placed in a safe deposit box. Why?"

As Rodeo started to get out of the car, he let out a big sigh and turned back to me, leaned over and said, "You should know the answer to that, MC. Cash does not leave a trail, paper, digital or electronic."

He just stared at me, and about that time I think one of my synapses must have popped and the light bulb finally went on.

Rodeo just smiled at me. Right before he got out of the car, he leaned back toward me and whispered, "Yep, that's right, Miss MC. Now go home and relax, and stop bugging Velma, so she'll leave me alone."

I watched him slide out, shut the door of my car, and disappear back into the bar where, no doubt, Ernie had a cold one waiting for him.

I slowly drove home to my condo. Up ahead, I could see Aunt Sophie and Aunt Anna out walking Harold's little yappy dogs and waving to me to come by. I decided I needed a hug and went up to meet them and have some spanakopita.

Besides, they would feed me, and if I was lucky, I would catch a glimpse of my mother out of the corner of my eye laughing her belly laugh and smiling at me. I could almost hear her now, *"You used up all your luck now with Tony, now get over to St. Mary's and bring lots of dollars."* And so, I did. One day, I grabbed a hefty amount of cash out of the safe deposit box; drove over to St. Mary's and placed it in the collection box for Saint Anthony.

I figured this would hold me over for a while. I went in and lit a candle at all the prayer stations and sat for a few minutes in a pew. I knew that someday I would leave this church for the last time and meet up with my mother across the shore. We would talk again like we used to, mama and daughter. Pick up where we left off.

I went back to the bank and took the remaining cash from the safe deposit box I had opened with the cash from Boris and stuffed it into the larger safe deposit box. There was just enough room for the bottle of ouzo. I then closed out the empty safe deposit box. After all, I was my mother's daughter. If it was good enough for Uncle Sam, it was good enough for me. After that, the light on my lamp was still for a little while.

## A NOTE TO THE READER

Dear Reader,

Thank you for reading my first book. I hope you enjoyed reading it and I hope you check out my other books. I would be most grateful if you would spread the word. Also, I hope you would take a minute or two to post an honest review on Amazon.

If you would like to chat, I would love to hear from you, so please feel free to email me at author@RitaMoreau.com. Drop by and visit me online at www.ritamoreau.com or www.facebook.com/RitaMoreauAuthor.

Until next time,

Rita

## ACKNOWLEDGMENTS

Rita Moreau is the author of WHODUNITS. She lives in Florida with her husband, George, who brags to everyone that he is the author's husband. He is much more. Without his motivation and help there would be no author.


Kathryn M. Stosius

10/24/1918 – 3/31/2014

I would like to acknowledge my deep gratitude to Kathryn Stosius. Kay was the first to explain to me how to go about bribing Saint Anthony. By 90 years young she was on a first name basis with Tony. She also taught me how to make a mean margarita.

Thank you, Kay. You were loved, and you are missed.

Made in the USA
Columbia, SC
25 May 2023

17272180R00146